WITHDRAWN

The Magic Christian

THE MAGIC CHRISTIAN

TERRY SOUTHERN

RANDOM HOUSE   NEW YORK

Second Printing

TO HENRY AND DIG

Little man whip a big man every time if the little man's in the right and keeps a'comin'.

MOTTO OF THE TEXAS RANGERS

The Magic Christian

I

When not tending New York holdings, Guy Grand was generally, as he expressed it, *"on the go."* He took cross-country trips by train: New York to Miami, Miami to Seattle—that sort of thing—always on a slow train, one that made frequent stops. Accommodation on these trains is limited, and though he did engage the best, Grand often had to be satisfied with a small compartment fitted with scarcely more than the essentials of comfort. But he accepted this cheerfully; and so today, on a summer afternoon at precisely 2:05, it was with buoyant step (considering his girth—for, at fifty-three now, he was rather stout) that he climbed aboard the first Pullman of the *Portland Plougher,* found his compartment, and began the pleasant routine of settling in for the long slow journey to New York. As was his habit, he immediately rang the porter to bring round a large bottle of Campari and a bottle of finely iced water; then he sat down at his desk to write business letters.

It was known that for any personal service Grand was inclined to tip generously, and because of this there were usually three or four porters loitering in the corridor nearby. They kept a sharp eye on the compartment door, in case Grand should signal some need or other; and, as the train pulled out of the station, they could hear him moving about inside, humming to himself, and shuffling papers to and fro on his desk. Before the train made its first stop, however, they would have to scurry, for Grand's orders were that the porters should not be seen when he came out of his compartment; and he did come out, at every stop.

At the first of these stops, which was not long in occurring, Grand went quickly to the adjoining day coach and took a seat by the window. There he was able to lean out and observe the activity on the platform; he attracted little attention himself, resembling as he did, with his pleasant red face, any honest farmer.

From the train window one could see over and beyond the station the rest of the small New England town—motionless now in the summer afternoon, like a toy mausoleum—while all that seemed to live within the town was being skillfully whipped underground and funneled up again in swift urgency onto the station platform, where small square cartons were unloaded from a central car.

But amidst the confusion and haste on the platform there was one recognizable figure; this was the man who sold hotdogs from a box he carried strapped to his neck.

"They're *red hot!*" he cried repeatedly, walking up and down parallel to the train and only a foot from it —while Grand, after a minute of general observation, focused all his attention on this person; and then, at exactly one minute before departure, he began his case with the hotdog-man.

"Red hot!" he shouted; and when the man reached the window, Grand eyed him shrewdly for a second, squinting, as though perhaps appraising his character, before asking, tight-lipped:

"*How much?*"

"Twenty cents," the hotdog-man said hurriedly— for the train was about to pull out—". . . mustard and relish, they're red hot!"

"Done!" said Grand with a sober nod, and as the train actually began to move forward and the hotdog-man to walk rapidly in keeping abreast of the window, Guy Grand leaned out and handed him a five-hundred-dollar bill.

"Break this?" he asked tersely.

The hotdog-man, in trying to utilize all their remaining time, passed the hotdog to Grand and reached into his change pocket before having looked carefully at the bill—so that by the time he made out its denomination, he was running almost full tilt, grimacing oddly and shaking his head, trying to return the bill with one hand and recover the hotdog with the other. During their final second together, with the hotdog-man's last overwhelming effort to reach his outstretched hand, Grand reached into his own coat pocket and took out a colorful plastic animal mask—today it was that of *pig*—which he quickly donned before beginning to gorge the hotdog through the mouth of the mask, at the same time reaching out frantically for the bill, yet managing somehow to keep it just beyond his fingers' grasp, and continuing with this while the distance between them lengthened, hopelessly, until at last the hotdog-man stood exhausted on the end of the platform, still holding the five hundred, and staring after the vanishing train.

When Grand finally drew himself back from the window and doffed his pig mask, it was to face a middle-aged woman across the aisle who was twisted halfway around in her seat, observing Grand with a curiosity so intense that the instant of their eyes actually meeting did not seem to register with her. Then she coughed and glanced away—but irresistibly back again, as Guy Grand rose, all smiles, to leave the day coach, giving the woman a wink of affectionate conspiracy as he did.

"Just having a laugh with that hot-frank vender," he explained. ". . . no real harm done, surely."

He returned to his compartment then, where he sat at the desk sipping his Campari—a drink the color of raspberries, but bitter as gall—and speculating about the possible reactions of the hotdog-man.

Outside the compartment, even at the far end of the corridor, the idle porters could often hear his odd chortle as he stirred about inside.

By the time the train reached New York, Guy Grand had gone through this little performance four or five times, curious fellow.

II

Out of the gray granite morass of Wall Street rises one building like a heron of fire, soaring up in blue-white astonishment—*Number 18 Wall*—a rocket of glass and blinding copper. It is the *Grand Investment Building*, perhaps the most contemporary business structure in our country, known in circles of high finance simply as *Grand's*.

Offices of *Grand's* are occupied by companies which deal in *mutual funds*—giant and fantastic corporations whose policies define the shape of nations.

August Guy Grand himself was a billionaire. He

had 180 millions cash deposit in New York banks, and this ready capital was of course but a part of his gross holdings.

In the beginning, Grand's associates, wealthy men themselves, saw nothing extraordinary about him; a reticent man of simple tastes, they thought, a man who had inherited most of his money and had preserved it through large safe investments in steel, rubber, and oil. What his associates managed to see in Grand was usually a reflection of their own dullness: a club member, a dinner guest, a possibility, a threat—a man whose holdings represented a prospect and a danger. But this was to do injustice to Grand's private life, because his private life was atypical. For one thing, he was the last of the big spenders; and for another, he had a very unusual attitude towards *people*—he spent about ten million a year in, as he expressed it himself, *"making it hot for them."*

*

At fifty-three, Grand had a thick trunk and a large balding bullet-head; his face was quite pink, so that in certain half-lights he looked like a fat radish-man —though not displeasingly so, for he always sported well-cut clothes and, near the throat, a diamond the size of a nickel . . . a diamond now that caught the late afternoon sun in a soft spangle of burning color when Guy stepped through the soundless doors of *Grand's* and into the blue haze of the almost empty street, past the huge doorman appearing larger than life in gigantic livery, he who touched his cap with quick but easy reverence.

"Cab, Mr. Grand?"

"Thank you no, Jason," said Guy, "I have the car today." And with a pleasant smile for the man, he turned adroitly on his heel, north towards Worth Street.

Guy Grand's gait was brisk indeed—small sharp steps, rising on the toes. It was the gait of a man who appears to be snapping his fingers as he walks.

Half a block on he reached the car, though he seemed to have a momentary difficulty in recognizing it; beneath the windshield wiper lay a big parking ticket, which Grand slowly withdrew, regarding it curiously.

"Looks like you've got a *ticket*, bub!" said a voice somewhere behind him.

Out of the corner of his eye Grand perceived the man, in a dark summer suit, leaning idly against the side of the building nearest the car. There was something terse and smug in the tone of his remark, a sort of nasal piousness.

11

"Yes, so it seems," mused Grand, without looking up, continuing to study the ticket in his hand. "How much will you eat it for?" he asked then, raising a piercing smile at the man.

"How's that, mister?" demanded the latter with a nasty frown, pushing himself forward a bit from the building.

Grand cleared his throat and slowly took out his wallet—a long slender wallet of such fine leather it would have been limp as silk, had it not been so chock-full of thousands.

"I asked what would you take to *eat* it? You know . . ." Wide-eyed, he made a great chewing motion with his mouth, holding the ticket up near it.

The man, glaring, took a tentative step forward.

"Say, I don't *get* you, mister!"

"Well," drawled Grand, chuckling down at his fat wallet, browsing about in it, "simple enough really . . ." And he took out a few thousand. "*I* have this ticket, as you know, and I was just wondering if you would care to *eat* it, for, say"—a quick glance to ascertain—"six thousand dollars?"

"What do you mean, '*eat it*?'" demanded the dark-suited man in a kind of a snarl. "Say, what're you anyway, bub, a *wise*-guy?"

" '*Wise*-guy' or '*grand* guy'—call me anything you like . . . as long as you don't call me '*late-for-chow!*'

Eh? Ho-ho." Grand rounded it off with a jolly chortle, but was quick to add, unsmiling, "How 'bout it, pal—got a taste for the easy green?"

The man, who now appeared to be openly angry, took another step forward.

"*Listen*, mister . . ." he began in a threatening tone, half clenching his fists.

"I think I should warn you," said Grand quietly, raising one hand to his breast, "that I am armed."

"*Huh?*" The man seemed momentarily dum-founded, staring down in dull rage at the six bills in Grand's hand; then he partially recovered, and cocking his head to one side, regarded Grand narrowly, in an attempt at shrewd skepticism, still heavily flavored with indignation.

"Just who do you think you *are*, Mister! Just what is your *game?*"

"Grand's the name, easy-green's the game," said Guy with a twinkle. "Play along?" He brusquely flicked the corners of the six crisp bills, and they crackled with a brittle, compelling sound.

"*Listen* . . ." muttered the man, tight-lipped, flex-ing his fingers and exhaling several times in angry exasperation, ". . . are *you* trying . . . are you try-ing to tell ME that you'll give *six thousand dollars* . . . to . . . to EAT that"—he pointed stiffly at the ticket in Guy's hand—"to *eat* that TICKET?!?"

"That's about the size of it," said Grand; he glanced at his watch. "It's what you might call a 'limited offer'—expiring in, let's say, *one minute.*"

"Listen, mister," said the man between clenched teeth, "if this is a gag, *so help me* . . ." He shook his head to show how serious he was.

"No threats," Guy cautioned, "or I'll shoot you in the temple—well, what say? Forty-eight seconds remaining."

"Let's *see* that goddamn money!" exclaimed the man, quite beside himself now, grabbing at the bills.

Grand allowed him to examine them as he continued to regard his watch. "Thirty-nine seconds remaining," he announced solemnly. "Shall I start the *big count down?*"

Without waiting for the latter's reply, he stepped back and, cupping his hands like a megaphone, began dramatically intoning, *"Twenty-eight . . . twenty-seven . . . twenty-six . . ."* while the man made several wildly gesticulated and incoherent remarks before seizing the ticket, ripping off a quarter of it with his teeth and beginning to chew, eyes blazing.

"Stout fellow!" cried Grand warmly, breaking off the count down to step forward and give the chap a hearty clap on the shoulder and hand him the six thousand.

"You needn't actually eat the ticket," he explained. "I was just curious to see if you had your price." He gave a wink and a tolerant chuckle. "Most of us have, I suppose. Eh? Ho-ho."

And with a grand wave of his hand, he stepped inside his car and sped away, leaving the man in the dark summer suit standing on the sidewalk staring after him, fairly agog.

III

Grand drove leisurely up the East River Drive—to a large and fine old house in the Sixties, where he lived with his two elderly aunts, Agnes and Esther Edwards.

He found them in the drawing room when he arrived.

"There you are, Guy!" said Agnes Edwards with tart affection, who at eighty-six was a year senior to Esther and held the initiative in most things between them.

"Guy, Guy, Guy," exclaimed Esther happily in her

turn, with a really beautiful pink smile for him—but she insisted then upon raising her teacup, so that all to be seen now was her brow, softly clouded, as ever, in maternal concern for the boy. Both women were terribly, chronically, troubled that Guy, at fifty-three, was unmarried—though perhaps each, in her way, would have fought against it.

Guy beamed at them from the doorway, then crossed to kiss both before going to his big sofa-chair by the window where he always sat.

"We're just having tea, darling—do!" insisted his Aunt Agnes with brittle passion, flourishing her little silver service bell in a smart tinkle and presenting her half-upturned face for his kiss—as though to receive it perfunctorily, but with eyelids closed and tremoring, one noticed, and a second very thin hand which, as in reflex, started to rise towards their faces, wavering up, clenched white as the lace at her wrists.

"Guy, Guy, Guy," cried Esther again, sharpening her own gaiety as she set her cup down—quickly enough, but with a care that gave her away.

"You will take tea, won't you, my Guy!" said Agnes, and she conveyed it in a glance to the maid who'd appeared.

"Love some," said Guy Grand, giving his aunts such a smile of fanatic brightness that they both squirmed a bit. He was in good spirits now after his trip—but soon enough, as the women could well attest, he would fall away from them, lapse into mystery behind his great gray *Financial Times* and *Wall Street Journal* for hours on end: distrait, they thought; never speaking, certainly; answering, yes—but most often in an odd and distant tone that told them nothing, nothing.

*

"Guy . . ." Agnes Edwards began, turning her cup in her hand and forcing one of the warm playful frowns used by the extremely rich to show the degree of seriousness felt.

"Yes, Aunt Agnes," said Guy unnecessarily, even brightly, actually coming forward a bit on his chair, not turning his own cup, but fingering it, politely nervous.

"Guy . . . you *know* Clemence's young man. Well, I *think* they want to get *married!* and . . . oh I don't know, I was just wondering if we couldn't *help*. Naturally, I haven't said a thing to her about it—I wouldn't dare, of course . . . but then what's *your* feeling on it, Guy? Surely there's something we can do, don't you agree?"

Guy Grand could have no notion what she was talking about, except that it was undoubtedly a question of money; but he spoke darkly enough to suggest that he was weighing his words with care.

"Why I should think so, yes."

Agnes Edwards beamed and raised her cup in a gesture both coy and smug, then the two women glanced at each other, smiling prettily, almost lifting their brows—whatever it was, it was a certain gain all around.

*

Grand's own idea of what he was doing—"making it hot for people"—had formed crudely, literally, and almost as an afterthought, when, early one summer morning in 1938, just about the time the Spanish Civil War was ending, he flew out to Chicago and, within an hour of arrival, purchased a property on one of the busiest corners of the Loop. He had the modern two-story structure torn down and the debris cleared off that day—that very morning, in fact—by a demolition crew of fifty men and machines; and then he directed the six carpenters, who had been on stand-by since early morning, when they had thrown up a plank barrier at the sidewalk, to construct the wooden forms for a concrete vat of the following proportions: fifteen feet square, five feet deep. This construction was done in an hour and a half, and it

seemed that the work, except for pouring the concrete, was ended; in fact the carpenters had put on
their street clothes and were ready to leave when,
after a moment of reflection, Grand assembled them
with a smart order to take down this present structure, and to rebuild it, but on a two-foot elevation—
giving clearance beneath, as he explained to the foreman, to allow for the installation of a heating apparatus there.

"That'll make it hot for them," he said—but he
wasn't speaking to the foreman then, nor apparently
to anyone else.

It was mid-afternoon, and collecting from the flux
of the swollen summer street were the spectators,
who hung in bunches at the sturdy barrier, gather-
ings in constant change, impressed in turn by the way
the great man from the East snapped his commands,
expensively dressed as he was, shirt turned back at
the cuff.

And when the work was going ahead correctly,
Grand might give the crowd a moment of surveillance from where he stood in the center of the lot,
finally addressing them, hands cupped to his mouth
as if he had to shout—though, actually, they were
only a few yards away.

"Tomorrow . . ." he would say, *". . . back . . .
tomorrow! Now . . . getting . . . it . . . ready!"*

When an occasional wiseacre could get his attention and attempt some joke as to what was going on there beyond the barrier, Grand Guy Grand would smile wearily and shake a scolding finger at him.

"Now . . . getting . . . it . . . ready," he would shout slowly, or something else equally irrelevant to the wiseacre's jibe; but no one took offense, either because of not understanding or else because of the dignity and bearing of the man, and the big diamond he wore at his throat.

Another contractor, three workers, a truck of sand and gravel, and six sacks of quick-drying cement arrived at the working site at two o'clock, but were forced to wait until the new forms were complete. Then a sheet of metal was lowered into place and the concrete was poured into the forms. Under Grand's spirited command, it was all so speedily done that well before dusk the work was ended, including the installation of a great gas burner there, star-shaped with a thousand dark jets, like a giant upturned squid stretched beneath the structure. It was apparent now that when the board forms were removed, the whole would resemble a kind of white stone bath, set on four short columns, with a heating apparatus beneath, and small ramps leading up the vat on each of its sides.

Before dinner Guy Grand completed arrangements

begun earlier in the day with the Chicago stockyards: these provided for the delivery of three hundred cubic feet of manure, a hundred gallons of urine, and fifty gallons of blood, to an address in the suburbs. Grand met them there and had the whole stinking mess transferred to a covered dump truck he had purchased that morning. These arrangements cost Grand a pretty penny, because the stockyards do not ordinarily conserve or sell urine, so that it had to be specially collected.

After securing the truck's cover, Grand climbed into the cab, drove back towards the stockyards and parked the truck there, where the stench of it would be less noticeable.

Then he took a taxi into town, to the near North Side and had a quiet dinner at the Drake.

At nine o'clock, while it was still light, he returned to the working site, where he was met by some of the crew, and saw to the removal of the board forms and the barrier. He inspected the vat, and the burner below—which he tested and found in good working order. Then he dismissed the crew and went back to his hotel.

He sat at his desk writing business letters until his thin gold wrist-clock sounded three A.M. Exactly then he put away his writing things, freshened himself up, and, just before leaving the room, paused near the door and collected a big leather brief case, a gas mask, a wooden paddle, a bucket of black paint, and an old, stiff paintbrush. He went downstairs and took a cab out to the place where he had parked the dump truck. Leaving the cab, he got into the truck and drove back to the working site. There he backed the truck carefully up one of the ramps and then emptied all that muck into the vat. The stench was nearly overpowering, and Grand, as soon as he had parked the truck and gotten out of it, was quick to don the gas mask he had brought.

Stepping up one of the ramps, he squatted on the parapet of the vat and opened the brief case, out of which he began taking, a handful at a time, and dropping into the vat, ten thousand one-hundred-dollar bills, slowly stirring them in with his wooden paddle.

And he was in this attitude, squatting at the edge of the vat, gas mask covering his face, stirring with his paddle and dumping bills into the muck, the work only half begun, when a passing police patrol car pulled up to investigate the activity and, above all, the stench. But before the officers could properly take account, Grand had closed the brief case, doffed his mask, given them five thousand dollars each, and demanded to be taken at once to their precinct captain. After a few hushed words between them, and a shrugging of shoulders, they agreed.

At the station, Grand spoke privately with the captain, showing him several business cards and explaining that it was all a harmless promotion stunt for a new product.

"Naturally my firm is eager to coöperate with the authorities," he said, and handed the captain twenty-five thousand.

And so it was finally agreed that Grand might return to the site and proceed, as long as whatever he was doing did not involve criminal violence within the precinct. Moreover, while the captain could make no definite promise about it, he was attentive enough to Grand's proposal of an additional fifty thousand on the following noon if the police would be kept away from the site for a few hours that morning.

"Think it over," said Grand pleasantly. "Better sleep on it, eh?"

Back at the site, Grand Guy donned his mask again, and dumped the remaining contents of the brief case into the vat. Then he stepped down, opened the can of paint, gave it good stirring, and finally, using his left hand so that what resulted looked childish or illiterate, he scrawled across the vat FREE $ HERE in big black letters on the sides facing the street.

He climbed up for a final check on the work. Of the bills in the muck, the corners, edges, and denomination figures of about five hundred were visible. After a moment he stepped down and, half crouching beneath the vat, took off his mask and saw to his burners. He did a short terse count down and turned the valve full open; then he removed the handle so that it could not easily be interfered with. As he touched off the match, the thousand flames sprang up, all blue light, and broke back doubling on the metal plate, and on the wet concrete—a color of sand in summer moonlight: one of those chosen instants, lost to childhood, damp places in reflection, surface of cement under the earth, the beautifully cool buried places . . . the stench became unbearable; he stood and quickly donned his mask, turned away from the site and walked across the street where he paused at the corner and surveyed the whole. Already in the pale eastern light, the moronic scrawl, FREE $ HERE, loomed with convincing force, while below the thousand flames beat up, blue-white and strangely urgent for this hour of morning on a down-town corner of Chicago.

"Say . . ." mused Grand, half-aloud, *"that'll* make it hot for them all right!" And he leaped into the big dump truck and drove like the wind back to his hotel. At dawn he caught the plane for New York.

The commotion that occurred a few hours later on that busy corner of the Loop in downtown Chicago was the first and, in a sense perhaps, the most deliberately literal of such projects eventually to be linked with the name of "Grand Guy" Guy Grand, provoking the wrath of the public press against him, and finally earning him the label, "Eccentric" and again towards the end, "Crackpot."

IV

"Is Clemence a person?" asked Guy, taking a bit of sweet biscuit now, popping it into his mouth.

Aunt Esther raised her hand to conceal a shaming twitter, and Aunt Agnes feigned impatience.

"Guy, great silly!" said Agnes. "Really!" Though after a moment she softened, to continue:

"Clemence is the new *maid!* She's a Catholic girl, Guy—*and* a very nice one, if I may say so. She's marrying this Jewish boy, Sol—how they'll manage I'm sure I don't know—I talked to them both, I told them that we were Protestants, had always been Protestants, and always *would* be Protestants—but that I didn't mind! Not in the least! 'Freedom of worship and creed!' I said. It's always been a principle of *my* religion. Not so insistent and pushy as *some* I could name! I didn't tell them *that*, of course, but there you are. Well, *she* wants a honeymoon in *Italy*, and a visit to the Pope, which I think is terribly sweet—and *he* wants to go to *his* place in the East, wherever it is; Israel, isn't it? Oh, I don't say it badly. They're *very* nice, Guy—both of them as gentle and polite as you please, and . . . well, they've enough money for *one* of the trips, you see, but *not* for both. I wish we could help them, Guy. I think it would be nice if they could go to *both* of their places, don't you agree? You remember how much I enjoyed Calvin's chair in Geneva! Of course it isn't the same, but it *would* be sweet. What's your feeling on it, Guy?"

"But Guy has always been *eager* to help in such matters," Esther broke in warmly.

"Thank you, Aunt Esther," said Guy with soft humility, "I do like to think that the record speaks for itself."

*

Guy Grand had owned a newspaper for a while—one of Boston's popular dailies, with a circulation of 900,-

ooo. When Grand assumed control, there was, at first, no change in the paper's format, nor in its apparently high journalistic standards, as Grand stayed on in New York on the periphery of the paper's operations, where he would remain, he said until he "could get the feel of things."

During the second month, however, French words began to crop up unaccountably in news of local interest:

Boston, Mar. 27 (AP)—Howard Jones, vingt-huit ans, convicted on three counts of larceny here, was sentenced this morning to 20-26 months in Folsom State Prison, Judge Grath of 17th Circuit Court of Appeals announced aujourd'hui.

Working then through a succession of editors, proofreaders, and linotype operators, Grand gradually put forward the policy of misspelling the names of cities, islands, and proper nouns in general—or else having them appear in a foreign language:

YANKS HIT PARIGI
MOP-UP AT TERWEEWEE

During the war, when geographic names were given daily prominence in the headlines, these distortions served to antagonize the reader and to obscure the facts.

The circulation of the paper fell off sharply, and after three months it was down to something less than one-twentieth of what it had been when Grand took over. At this point a major policy change was announced. Henceforth the newspaper would not carry comics, editorials, feature stories, reviews, or advertising, and would present only the factual news in a straightforward manner. It was called *The Facts*, and Grand spent the ransom of a dozen queens in getting at the facts of the news, or at least a great many of them, which he had printed then in simple sentences. The issues of the first two days or so enjoyed a fair sale, but the contents on the whole appeared to be so incredible or so irrelevant that by the end of the week demand was lower than at any previous phase of the paper's existence. During the third week, the paper had no sale at all to speak of, and was simply given away; or, refused by the distributors, it was left in stacks on the street corners each morning, about two million copies a day. In the beginning people were amused by the sight of so many newspapers lying around unread; but when it continued, they became annoyed. Something funny was going on—*Communist? Atheist? Homosexual? Catholic? Monopoly? Corruption? Protestant? Insane? Ne-*

gro? Jewish? Puerto Rican? POETRY? The city was filthy. It was easy for people to talk about *The Facts* in terms of litter and debris. Speeches were made, letters written, yet the issue was vague. The editor of *The Facts* received insulting letters by the bagful. Grand sat tight for a week, then he gave the paper over exclusively to printing these letters; and its name was changed again—*Opinions.*

These printed letters reflected such angry divergence of thought and belief that what resulted was sharp dissension throughout the city. Group antagonism ran high. The paper was widely read and there were incidents of violence. Movements began.

*

At about two P.M. on June 7th, crowds started to gather in Lexington Square near the center of the city. The *Jewish, Atheist, Negro, Labor, Homosexual,* and *Intellectual* groups were on one side—the *Protestant* and *American Legion* on the other. The balance of power, or so it seemed, lay with the doughty *Catholic* group.

It was fair and windless that day in Boston, and while the groups and the groups-within-groups bickered and jockeyed in the center of Lexington Square, Guy Grand brought off a *tour de force.*

Hovering just overhead, in a radio-equipped helicopter, he directed the maneuver of a six-plane squadron of skywriters, much higher, in spelling out the mile-long smoke-letter words: F**K YOU . . . and this was immediately followed by a veritable host of outlandish epithets, formulated as insults on the level of group Gestalt: Protestants are assholes . . . Jews are full of crap . . . Catholics are shitty . . . and so on, *ad nauseum* actually.

It set the crowd below hopping mad. Grand Guy Grand dropped to about a hundred feet, where he canted the plane towards them and opened the door to peer out and observe. The crowd, associating the low-flying helicopter with the outrageous skywriting going on above, started shouting obscenities and shaking their fists.

"You rotten Mick!"

"You dirty Yid!"

"You black bastard!"

That was how the fighting began.

During the Lexington Square Riots, Grand set his plane down to twenty-five feet, where he cruised around, leaning out the door, expressionless, shouting in loud, slow intonation:

"WHAT'S . . . UP? WHAT'S . . . UP?"

*

By four o'clock the square was in shambles and all Boston on the brink of eruption. The National Guard had to be brought into the city and martial law obtained. It was thirty-six hours before order was fully restored.

The press made capital of the affair. Investigations were demanded. Guy Grand had paid off some big men in order to carry forward the project, but this was more than they had bargained for. Back in New York it cost him two million to keep clear.

V

"Yes, I see," said Guy, clearing his throat, looking with concern at the piece of sweet biscuit in his hand, ". . . certainly. Why don't you . . . well, you know, find out how much they need, make out a check, and . . ."

Aunt Esther covertly twittered again, her eyes bright above the very white hand that hid her mouth, and Agnes turned her own face sharply away in mock exasperation with the boy.

"Not *give* them the money, Guy!" Agnes exclaimed.

"They wouldn't *hear* of it, of course—the young man, *Sol*, especially. Surely you know how *proud* those people are . . . a defensive-mechanism, I suppose; but there you are, even so! *No*—what I had in mind was to tell them of a *stock* to buy, you see."

"Right," said Guy crisply, "then they would take one of the trips later, that the idea? But, hold on— if they spend all their money on the one trip, how can they buy into the stock in question?"

"Guy!" said his aunt in a voice of ice and pain.

"I'm afraid I don't follow," said Grand with perfect candor.

Aunt Esther took refuge behind her kerchief, into her ceaseless giggling.

"*I mean make it go up and down!*" cried Agnes crossly. "Or rather *down* first, then *up*."

She regarded him narrowly for a moment, her thinness stretching upwards like an angry swan, suspecting perhaps that he was being deliberately obtuse.

"A perfect babe in the woods!" she said. "How you manage to hold your own at conference table I'm sure I couldn't imagine!"

"Sorry," said Grand, unsmiling, following through with the youthful gesture of slightly ducking his head for a sip of tea.

Of course it was all largely an act between them.

"Name one good stock in which you hold ten thousand shares," said Agnes sharply.

"One good stock . . ." repeated Guy Grand, his great brow clouding.

". . . that begins with an 'A'," said Aunt Esther.

"That begins with an 'A'?" said Grand, almost incredulous, yet as willing as a good-natured child at play.

"Esther!" cried Agnes.

"Well, do you mean *exactly* ten thousand, or *at least* ten thousand?" asked Guy.

"At least ten thousand," said Agnes. "And it *needn't*," she added, with a straight look to her sister, "begin with an 'A'!"

"Hmm. Well, how about 'Abercrombie and Adams'?" said Grand tentatively, "there's a fairly sound—"

"Good," said Aunt Agnes. "Now then, what if you sold all your shares of that? What would happen to the price of it?"

"Take a nasty drop," said Grand, with a scowl at the thought of it. "Might cause a run."

"There you are then!" cried Agnes. "And Clemence's young man *buys*—when the price is down, *he buys*, you see—then the *next* day, you buy back what you sold! I should think it would go up again when you buy back what you sold, wouldn't it?"

"Might and might not," said Grand, somewhat coldly.

"*Well,*" said Agnes, with a terrible hauteur, "you can just *keep* buying until it does!" Then she continued, in softer tones, to show her ultimate reasonableness: "Surely you can, Guy. And then, you see, when it's up again, Clemence and her young man will *sell.*"

"Yes," said Grand with a certain quiet dignity, "but you know, it might not look good, that sort of thing, with the Federal Securities Commission."

Agnes's lips were so closely compressed now that they resembled a turtle's mouth.

"Might not *look,*" she repeated, making it hollow, her eyes widening as though she had lifted a desert rock and seen what was beneath it. "*Well,*" she said with unnerving softness, taking a sip of tea to brace herself and even turning to draw on her sister with a look of dark significance, ". . . if all you're concerned with is *appearance*—then perhaps you aren't the person I thought you were, after all." And she poured herself another cup.

Grand was stricken with a mild fit of coughing. "Yes," he was able to say at last, ". . . yes, I see your point, of course. Does bear some thinking through though, I must say."

His aunt, momentarily aghast, had just started to

speak again, when the maid stepped inside the door to announce the arrival of Miss Ginger Horton—an extremely fat lady, who entered the room then, wearing an immense trapeze sunsuit and carrying her Pekinese.

"*Guy!*" she cried, extending her hand, as he, rising, came forward. "How *too* good to see you!

"Say hello to *Guy*, my Bitsy!" she shrieked gaily to the dog, pointing him at Guy and the others. "Say hello to everybody! There's Agnes and Esther, *see* them, Bitsy?"

The dog yapped crossly instead, and ran at the nose.

"*Is* Bitsy-witsy sicky?" cooed Miss Horton, pouting now as she allowed Guy to slowly escort her towards a chair near the others, he maneuvering her across the room like a gigantic river scow. "Hmm? Is my Bitsy sicky-wicky?"

"Nothing too serious, I hope," said Grand with a solicitous frown.

"Just nerves I expect," said Miss Horton, haughty now, and fairly snapping. "The weather is just so . . . *really abominable,* and then all the nasty little people about . . . Now here's your Agnes and Esther, Bitsy."

"How very nice to see you, my dear," said the two elderly women, each laying thin fingers on her enormous hand. "What an adorable little sunsuit! It *was* kind of you to bring your Bitsy—wasn't it, Guy?"

"It was extremely kind," said Guy, beaming as he retreated to his own great chair near the window.

*

It was, as a matter of fact, Guy Grand who, working through his attorneys, had bought controlling interest in the three largest kennel clubs on the eastern seaboard last season; and in this way he had gained virtual dominance over, and responsibility for, the Dog Show that year at Madison Square Garden. His number-one *gérant,* or front man, for this operation was a Señor Hernandez Gonzales, a huge Mexican, who had long been known in dog-fancier circles as a breeder of blue-ribbon Chihuahuas. With Grand's backing however, and over a quick six months, Gonzales became the celebrated owner of one of the finest kennels in the world, known now not simply for Chihuahuas, but for Pekinese, Pomeranians and many rare and strange breeds of the Orient.

It was evident that this season's show at the Garden was to be a gala one—a wealth of new honors had been posted, the prize-money packets substantially fattened, and competition was keener than ever. Bright young men and wealthy dowagers from all over were bringing forward their best and favorite pedigrees. Gonzales himself had promised a prize specimen of a fine old breed. A national picture magazine devoted its cover to the affair and a lengthy editorial in praise of this great American benignity, this love of animals—". . . in bright and telling contrast," the editorial said, "to certain naïve barbarities, *e.g.*, the Spanish bullfight."

Thus, when the day arrived, all was as it should be. The Garden was festively decked, the spectators in holiday reverence, the lights burning, the big cameras booming, and the participants dressed as for a Papal audience—though slightly ambivalent, between not wishing to get mussed or hairy, and yet wanting to pamper and coo over their animals.

Except for the notable absence of Señor Gonzales, things went smoothly, until the final competition began, that between "Best of Breed" for the coveted "Best in Show." And at this point, Gonzales did appear; he joined the throng of owners and beasts who mingled in the center of the Garden, where it was soon apparent his boast had not been idle—at the end of the big man's leash was an extraordinary dog; he was jet-black and almost the size of a full-grown Dane, with the most striking coat and carriage yet seen at the Garden show that season. The head was dressed somewhat in the manner of a circus-cut poodle, though much exaggerated, so that half the face of the animal was truly obscured.

Gonzales joined the crowd with a jaunty smile and flourish not inappropriate to one of his eminence. He hadn't been there a moment though before he and the dog were spotted by Mrs. Winthrop-Garde and her angry little spitz.

She came forward, herself not too unlike her charge, waddling aggressively, and she was immediately followed by several other women of similar stamp, along with Pekineses, Pomeranians, and ill-tempered miniature chows.

Gonzales bowed with winning old-world grace and caressed the ladies' hands.

"What a *perfect* love he is!" shrieked Mrs. Winthrop-Garde of the animal on Gonzales's leash, and turning to her own, "*Isn't* he, my darling? *Hmm? Hmm?* Isn't he, my precious sweet? And what*ever* is his *name?*" she cried to Gonzales when her own animal failed to respond, but yapped crossly instead.

"He is called . . . *Claw*," said Gonzales with a certain soft drama which may have escaped Mrs. Winthrop-Garde, for she rushed on, heedless as ever.

"*Claude!* It's *too* delicious—the perfect darling! Say *hello* to Claude, Angelica! Say *hello* to Claude, my fur-flower!"

And as she pulled the angry little spitz forward,

while it snapped and snorted and ran at the nose, an extraordinary thing happened—for what this Grand and Gonzales had somehow contrived, and for reasons never fathomed by the press, was to introduce in disguise to the Garden show that season not a dog at all, but some kind of terrible black panther or dyed jaguar—hungry he was too, and cross as a pickle—so that before the day was out, he had not only brought chaos into the formal proceedings, but had actually destroyed about half the "Best of Breed."

During the first hour or so, Gonzales, because of his respected position in that circle, was above reproach, and all of the incidents were considered as being accidental, though, of course, extremely unfortunate.

"Too much spirit," he kept explaining, frowning and shaking his head; and, as he and the beast stalked slowly about in the midst of the group, he would chide the monster-cat:

"Overtired from the trip, I suppose. Isn't that it, boy? *Hmm? Hmm?*"

So now occasionally above the yapping and whining, the crowd would hear a strange *swish!* and *swat!* as Gonzales and the fantastic beast moved on, flushing them one by one.

Finally one woman, new to the circle, who did not

know how important Gonzales was, came back with an automatic pistol and tried to shoot the big cat. But she was so beside herself with righteous fury that she missed and was swiftly arrested.

Gonzales, though, apparently no fool himself, was quick to take this as a cue that his work was done, and he gradually retired, so that "Best in Show" was settled at last, between those not already eliminated.

Grand later penned a series of scathing articles about the affair: "Scandal of the Dog Show!" "Can This Happen Here?" "Is It Someone's Idea of a Joke?" etc., etc.

The bereft owners were wealthy and influential people, more than eager to go along with the demand for an inquiry. As quickly as witnesses were uncovered, however, they were bought off by Grand or his representatives, so that nothing really ever came of it in the end—though, granted, it did cost him a good bit to keep his own name clear.

VI

"And how was your *trip*, Guy?" asked Ginger Horton, sniffing a bit, just to be on the safe side it seemed.

Guy shrugged.

"Oh, same old six-and-seven, Ginger," he said.

"I beg your pardon," interjected his Aunt Agnes smartly.

Esther beamed, truly in league at last with her long-dead favorite sister's only son.

"It means *not too good*, Agnes," she said emphatically. "It's an expression used in dice-playing: You 'come out'—isn't that right, Guy?—on 'six,' your *point,* then you throw, in this case, a *'seven,'* which means: *no good, you* lose." She looked to her Guy. "That's it, isn't it, dear?"

"Oh, it's a *gambling* expression," said Agnes Edwards with a certain amused complacency, though she must have raised her cup rather too hurriedly, for Esther was content merely to beam at Guy.

"Then your trip wasn't . . . *too good,* is that it?" asked Ginger Horton seriously, setting her own cup down squarely, pressing the napkin briefly to her lips.

Esther started to answer, but in the end looked to Guy instead.

"Oh, it's just a manner of speaking," said Guy Grand easily. "What really gives the expression bite, of course, is that *six* is generally an easy point to make, you see, and, well . . . but then the fact is really, that the . . . uh, the *national economy,* so to speak, isn't in the best of shape just now. Not a buyer's market at all really. A bit bearish as a matter of fact." He gave a chuckle, looking at the Pekinese.

Ginger Horton seized the opportunity to bring the dog into it.

"Well, it's all over *our* head, isn't it, Bitsy? Hmm? Isn't it over your Bitsy-witsy head? Hmmm?"

"*Bearish* . . ." Esther began to explain.

"I think we all know what *that* means, Esther," said Agnes shortly, raising one hand to her throat, her old eyes glittering no less than the great diamonds she clutched there.

*

Evidently Grand liked playing the donkey-man. In any case, he had bought himself a large motion-picture house in Philadelphia. The house had been losing money badly for six months, so it was natural that the manager and his staff, who knew nothing of Grand's background, should be apprehensive over the probable shake-up.

The manager was a shrewd and capable man of many years' experience in cinema management, a man whose position represented for him the fruit of a life's work. He decided that his best move, under the circumstances, would be to go to Grand and cheerfully recommend salary cuts for all.

During their first conference, however, it was Grand, in his right as new owner, who held the initiative throughout.

By way of preliminary, and while the manager sat alertly on the edge of a big leather chair, Grand paced the floor of the comfortable office, his hands clasped at his back, and a slight frown on his face. Finally he stopped in the center of the room and addressed the manager:

"The *Chinese* have an expression, Mr. . . . *Mister Manager*. I believe it occurs in the book of the *I Ching:* "Put your house in order," they say, "*that* is the first step.""

This brought a flush to the manager's face and caused him to shift in his chair.

"My dad," said Grand then, and with severe reverence, "pushed out here in . . . 1920. There were few frontiers open for him at that time. There are fewer still . . . open-for-us-today!"

He faced the manager and would have let him speak; in fact, by looking straight into his face, he invited him to do so, but the man could only nod in sage agreement.

"If there is one unexplored territory," Grand continued, waxing expansive now, "one virgin wood alive today in this man's land of ours—it is cinema management! My dad—"Dad Grand"—was a championship golfer. That *may* be why . . . now this is only a guess . . . but that *may* be why he always favored the maxim: 'If you want them to play your course—don't put rocks on the green!' "

Grand paused for a minute, staring down at the manager's sparkling shoes as he allowed his great brow to furrow and his lips to purse, frantically pensive. Then he shot a question:

"Do you know the story of the Majestic Theatre in Kansas City?"

The manager, a man with thirty years' experience in the field, who knew the story of every theatre in the country, did not know this one.

"In August, 1939, the management of the K.C. Majestic changed hands, *and* policy. Weston seats were installed—four inches wider than standard—and 'a.p.'s,' admission prices, were cut in half . . . and two people were to occupy each seat. The new manager, Jason Frank, who died of a brain hemorrhage later the same year, had advanced Wyler Publicity nine hundred dollars for the catch-phrase, 'Half the Price, and a Chance for Vice,' which received a wide private circulation."

Grand broke off his narrative to give the manager a searching look before continuing:

". . . *but* it didn't work, sir! It *did not* work . . . and I'll tell you why: it was a *crackpot* scheme. A crackpot scheme, and rocks on the green! It cost Frank his licence, his health, and in this case perhaps his very life."

Grand paused for effect and crossed to the desk where he took up a sheaf of onionskin papers and threshed them about before the manager. Each sheet was black with figures.

"According to my figures," he said tersely, "this house will fold in nine months' time unless there is, at minimum, an eight percent climb in 'p.a.'s'—paid admissions." Here he frowned darkly, let it pass, forced a smile, and then flapped his arms a time or two, as he resumed speaking, in a much lighter tone now:

"Of course there are a number of . . . of *possibilities* for us here . . . I have certain plans . . . oh granted they're tentative, under wrap, irons in the fire, if you like—but I *can* tell you *this:* I am retaining you and your staff. We are not ploughing the green under. Do you follow? Right. Now I have arranged for this increase in your salaries: ten percent. I won't say it is a *substantial* increase; I say simply: *ten percent* . . . which means, of course, that all . . . *all these figures*"—he waved the sheaf of papers in a gesture of hopelessness and then dropped them into the wastebasket—"will have to be *revised!* More time lost before we know where we stand! Yet that can't be helped. It *is* a move—and *I* say it is a move . . . in the right direction!"

He spoke to the manager for an hour, thinking aloud, getting the feel of things, keeping his hand in, and so on. Then he dismissed him for three months' paid vacation.

Grand's theatre was one of the city's largest and

had first-run rights on the most publicized films. In the manager's absence, things proceeded normally for a while; until one night when the house was packed for the opening of the smart new musical, *Main Street, U. S. A.*

First there was an annoying half-hour delay while extra camp-stool seats were sold and set up in the aisles; then, when the house lights finally dimmed into blackness, and the audience settled back to enjoy the musical, Grand gave them something they weren't expecting: a cheap foreign film.

The moment the film began, people started leaving. In the darkness, however, with seats two-abreast choking the aisles, most of them were forced back. So the film rolled on; and while the minutes gathered into quarter-hours, and each quarter-hour cut cripplingly deep into the evening, Grand, locked in the projection room high above, stumbled from wall to wall, choking with laughter.

After forty-five minutes, the film was taken off and it was announced over the public-address system, and at a volume strength never before used anywhere, that a mistake had been made, that this was *not* the new musical.

Shouts of *"And how!"* came from the crowd, and *"I'll say it's not!"* and *"You're telling me! God!"*

Then after another delay for rewinding, the cheap

foreign film was put on again, upside down.

By ten thirty the house was seething towards angry panic, and Grand gave the order to refund the money of everyone who wished to pass by the box office. At eleven o'clock there was a line outside the theatre two blocks long.

From his office above, Grand kept delaying the cashier's work by phoning every few minutes to ask: "How's it going?" or "What's up?"

The next day there was a notice on the central bulletin board:

"Rocks on the green! All hands alert!"

It also announced another fat pay-hike.

Into certain films such as *Mrs. Miniver*, Grand made eccentric inserts.

In one scene in *Mrs. Miniver*, Walter Pidgeon was sitting at evening in his fire-lit study and writing in his journal. He had just that afternoon made the acquaintance of Mrs. Miniver and was no doubt thinking about her now as he paused reflectively and looked towards the open fire. In the original version of this film, he took a small penknife from the desk drawer and meditatively sharpened the pencil he had been writing with. During this scene the camera re-mained on his *face*, which was filled with quiet re-flection and modest hopefulness, so that the intended emphasis of the scene was quite clear: his genteel and wistfully ambitious thoughts about Mrs. Miniver.

The insert Grand made into this film, was, like those he made into others, professionally done, and as such, was technically indiscernable. It was introduced just at the moment where Pidgeon opened the knife, and it was a three-second close shot of the fire-glint blade.

This simple insert misplaced the emphasis of the scene; the fire-glint blade seemed to portend dire evil, and occurring as it did early in the story, simply "spoiled" the film.

Grand would hang around the lobby after the show to overhear the remarks of those leaving, and often he would join in himself:

"What was that part about the *knife?*" he would demand querulously, stalking up and down the lobby, striking his fist into his open hand, ". . . he *had* that knife . . . I thought he was going to try and *kill* her! Christ, I don't *get* it!"

In some cases, Grand's theatre had to have two copies of the film on hand, because his alterations were so flagrant that he did not deem it wise to project the altered copy twice in succession. This was the case with a popular film called *The Best Years of Our Lives.* This film was mainly concerned, in its attempt at an odd kind of realism, with a young veteran of war, who was an amputee and had metal hooks instead of hands. It was a story told quite seriously and one which depended for much of its drama upon a straight-faced identification with the amputee's situation and attitude. Grand's insert occurred in the middle of the film's big scene. This original scene was a seven-second pan of the two principal characters, the amputee and his pretty home-town fiancée while they were sitting on the family porch swing one summer evening. The hero was courting her, in his quiet way—and this consisted of a brave smile, more or less in apology, it would seem, for having the metal hooks instead of hands—while the young girl's eyes shone with tolerance and understanding . . . a scene which was interrupted by Grand's insert: a cut to below the girl's waist where the hooks were seen to hover for an instant and then disappear, grappling urgently beneath her skirt. The duration of this cut was less than one-half second, but was unmistakably seen by anyone not on the brink of sleep.

It brought some of the audience bolt upright. Others the scene affected in a sort of double-take way, reacting to it as they did only minutes later. The rest, that is to say about one-third of the audience, failed to notice it at all; and the film rolled on. No one could believe his eyes; those who were positive they had seen something funny in the realism there, sat through the film again to make certain—

though, of course, the altered version was never run twice in succession—but *all* who had seen were so obsessed by what they had seen, or what they imagined they had seen, that they could no longer follow the story line, though it was, from that point on, quite as it was intended, without incongruity or surprise.

Grand had a good deal of trouble about his alterations of certain films and was eventually sued by several of the big studios. You can bet it cost him a pretty to keep clear in the end.

VII

"My Lord Russell books came today," said Ginger Horton, suddenly dropping her voice to a stage whisper, because the dog in her lap seemed to have gone asleep.

"*Pardon*," said Grand, almost shouting.

Mrs. Horton, dramatically wide-eyed now, raised a finger to her lips.

"*I think Bitsy's asleep*," she cooed, then stole a glance at the dog. "Isn't it *too* sweet!" she said, lifting her face to the others, beaming angelically.

"Oh, it *is* too sweet!" agreed Agnes and Esther, craning forward to see, like ancient things stretching across the sand. "Guy," hissed Agnes, "do come and see!"

"Best not," said Guy sagely, "might wake it."

"Guy's right," said Ginger Horton, compressing her lips tersely and cautioning the two ladies back. "Oh, how cross my Bitsy'd be. You *are* sweet, Guy," she added, with a piercing smile for him—but before he could acknowledge it with one of his own, she let a look of great care return to her face.

"I was *saying* that my Lord Russell books came today."

"Lord Russell?" Guy inquired genially.

"Laird K. Russell," murmured Esther in pure wonder as some dear forgotten name loomed up to marvel her softly from the far far away.

"*Bertrand Russell!*" exclaimed Agnes sharply, "the philosopher! Good heavens, Esther!"

"Not Bertrand Russell," cried Ginger Horton, "Lord Russell of Liverpool. The atrocity books!"

"Good Heavens," said Agnes.

"Well, do you know what we did?" Ginger Horton demanded. "Bitsy and I sat right down and pretended that *this* . . . *this* . . . *Thorndike* had been *captured* and brought to justice and all those atrocities had been done to him! To him and to a lot of other nasty little people we could think of!"

"Gracious," exclaimed Agnes.

"Not *Bill* Thorndike surely?" said Grand, coming forward on his chair with a show of concern.

"Oh, it's just absolutely *maddening!*" said Ginger Horton. "I don't even want to . . . to *talk* about it. Not in front of Bitsy, anyway."

"The dog?" said Grand. "It's asleep, isn't it?"

"Bitsy knows, of course," said Miss Horton darkly, ignoring this, "and only too well!"

"Ginger," said Agnes, "can you really be so sure of that?"

"Oh, in simply a thousand-thousand ways," said Ginger Horton.

"Do you remember that young Mr. Laird K. Russell?" asked Esther of Agnes in the pause that followed. "He came to our Westport summer ball for little Nancy."

"Great Heavens, Esther, that was over sixty years ago! Surely you don't mean it!"

Esther nodded, her eyes dim with distant marvel, a pale smile on her lips.

"Esther, really!"

Ginger Horton sniffed, at no pains to hide her annoyance with this change of focus, while Agnes tried to recover the thread.

"Do have more tea, Ginger—and please tell us wherever *did* you get that darling little sunsuit? How perfectly clever it is!"

"You *are* sweet, Agnes," said Ginger, brightening, yet seeming to imply a moment of reproach for Esther and Guy before turning her attention to the great pink tent of a sunsuit she was wearing.

"Yes, I think it's fun, don't you? Of course Charles did it for me."

"Simply too adorable!" said Agnes. "Isn't it, Guy?"

"It's extremely attractive," said Guy in most richly masculine and persuasive tones, and the ladies beamed all around.

*

One of Guy Grand's sayings at conference was this:

"Show me the man who's above picking up bits and pieces—and *I'll* show *you:* a fool!"

Just so, Grand himself kept his finger in more than one peripheral pie. In 1950 he bought out Vanity Cosmetics, a large and thriving Fifth Avenue concern. He surprised staffers at Vanity by bringing in his own research chemists, from allied fields. But these staff executives, all old-timers themselves, were only waiting for reassurance, and it wasn't long in coming when Grand spoke of fresh blood, new horizons, and thinking big.

"You've got to look ahead in this man's game," he

emphasized at first conference, "or by jumbo you're up crap creek without a paddle!"

Granted he spoke harshly, but in his tone was tough jaunty conviction and brutal know-how.

"He's all right," said one Vanity staffer after the session. "He speaks his mind, and devil take the hindmost!"

"Joe, he's my kinda guy," another was quick to agree. ". . . I mean what the hell, we're *all* out for money—am I right, Joe?"

These regulars though, were more or less cut off from lab contact now, as Grand told them he wanted to "go it alone for a bit."

"*Just* want to see how the land lies," he said.

He worked tirelessly with his new chemists, himself clad in a great white smock, bustling about the lab, seeing to this test and that result.

"Back in harness!" he liked to say at conference (for it was his habit to go there wearing his smock), and it made the others feel a bit inadequate—spic and span as they were in their smart tweeds and clergy gray—while the new chief sat stained and pungent from the lab.

"You civies have a soft touch here," Grand would tweak them—though of course they were only too eager now to go to the lab themselves.

63

"You know I wouldn't mind a crack at the lab," one of the senior exec's would say with serious mien if he could get Grand aside.

"Yes, I'll just bet you wouldn't," Grand would reply with a glittering smile, "and how about a handful of these while you're at it?" and he would flash a fat roll of ten thousands that he could just get into the catch-all pocket of his big white smock.

Though the exec might suspect that Grand was speaking symbolically, the gambit was always impressive.

"*Yes, sir,*" would be the earnest reply, "I really *would* like a crack at the lab!"

But Grand would grimace oddly and wave a finger at the senior staffer; then he would give a thin cackling laugh and fly to his flasks and beakers.

"The old boy's sharp as a razor," most of them said. "He's my kinda guy."

What happened in the end was the development of a couple of fairly new products. The first was *Downy,* a combination shampoo and soft-set; and it was heralded by a large-scale promotional campaign. The formula of *Downy* was supposedly based on a principle used by the Egyptians in the preservation of their dead—though this was but vaguely referred to, being simply the scientific springboard for the product and thereby catching the endorsement of men in various fields, and gaining press coverage beyond mere paid advertisement. The main promotional emphasis though was on the social allure and overall security it seemed to promise. "DOWNY," according to these releases, *will make your hair . . . softer than the hair of* YOUR OWN CHILD!"

It was unconditionally guaranteed to do so. These releases went on to present certain inductive proofs that the formula of *Downy* had been "Cleopatra's secret," that in reality she had been a woman of "only average prettiness (*which one must never never underestimate*)" and that she had won her thrones and her men with "what is *now* YOUR OWN . . . D O W N Y."

The promotional campaign was in progress for quite a while before the product was offered to the general buyer, though it had of course been used with amazing success for a long time by a number of famous beauties, and there were plenty of testimonials to that effect. So that when it was finally offered, the sales ran high indeed.

"I think we've hit on something here," said the smock-stained veteran, Grand Guy Grand, at conference with the staffers as the market tabulations poured in that first morning. "I *don't* like to count the chickens so to speak, but *I think* we've hit on something here . . . something that may well spell 'touchdown' in the hearts of Mr. and Mrs. U.S.A.!"

The others were agreeing wildly, but Grand was quick to show conference acumen, ". . . *not* count the chickens, I say"—and he raised a cautionary finger—"*nor* put all in *one basket!*"

And even as he hinted at research for another new product already under way, adverse reports about the soft-set began coming in by the carload. For what this Grand Guy in his work with the new chemists had contrived was a potion that did *not* soften the hair, after all, but on the contrary, made it *all stiff and wiry*.

As the reports flooded in, along with an avalanche of lawsuits, staffers at the conference table grew restive.

"Well, can't win 'em all," said Grand with a good loser's chuckle. "Common Zen savvy tells us as much," and he was content to dismiss the product's failure with this, eager now to get started on something new; but as it became ever more apparent that their million-dollar planning had gone so terribly wrong, the staffers got panicky.

"We do our best," said Grand, shaking his head stoically. "No man can say more."

It appeared though that one of the senior execs, a white-haired man of about forty-two, might actually jump out the window.

Grand, who held the initiative throughout most of the conferences, quietly led the man back to the table, and summed up in this way:

"Talk is cheap, gentlemen, and since I'm not one personally to favor tired phrases, I *think* I'll spare you the grand old maxim about 'spilt milk,' but I do want to say this: Show me the man who *looks back* —and *I'll* show *you:* a first-rate imbecile!"

This brought conference around, and under Grand's good guidance, they ignored the raging anathema without and looked to the future.

"Our M.R. people have come up with something," said Grand, "—that's what we pay them for—well, they've come up with a couple of consumer principles we can kick around here at conference: one, the insatiate craving of the public for an *absolute;* and two, the modern failure of monotheism—that is to say, the *failure* of the notion that *any absolute* can be presented as one separate thing."

Grand paused to touch his fingers together before him, shooting sharply evaluative looks at several staffers nearest before he continued:

"And they're quite right, of course. We of the . . . the extreme occident, for right or wrong—and there I've said it myself—think in *dichotomies* . . . have done so since our very inception. Oneness? Never had a chance in this great land of ours! Well, I ask you staffers, where does that leave us? Monotheism shot to pieces on the one hand—dire craving for an absolute existing on the other. I submit to you staffers that the solution establishes itself before our very eyes: namely, that an *absolute*—in any particular field—must be presented as a *dichotomy!* Yes, if one mother company, such as our Vanity, could confront the public with a *pure dichotomy,* in any particular product, it would gain virtual monopoly there. Yes, and *we* will present such a dichotomy! Two sides which embrace the extremes and meet in the middle! I say people will make their choice *within* the dichotomy presented by the mother company; they will not go outside it, because then the issue would become vague and the implications of the choice no longer clear and satisfying . . . *satisfying* in terms, I mean to say, of the self-orientation for which they *do,* in the last analysis, buy these products at all. Are there any dissensions from the view I've expressed?"

There were none to speak of and Grand continued briefly:

"Now what we want is one product which we can present in the two forms—good and evil, old and new, primitive and civilized—two items designed for the same use but presented as completely antithetical, both morally and philosophically—not aesthetically, however . . . packaging will be high-tone and identical, let the departments concerned take note . . . now do any of you—execs, staffers—know what that product might be?"

They did not, but this was evidently just a teaser anyhow, for Grand had already selected his product, and the work on it even now was under way. It was to be a body deodorant of course—presented, as he had suggested, in two forms. The first was traditional, combining the clinical and the erotic, offering, as it did, ". . . *Protection for Those Most Precious Moments of All—It Cuts Away Body Odor like a Knife.*" It was technically superior to any others on the market, making use of ". . . liquid glass, harmless plastic sealers . . ." and so on. It was called *Stealth.* The second deodorant was based on another principle altogether, *biology.* An ancient wisdom revived, it had to do with natural selection among mating animals, and did, according to eminent and quoted authorities, rest securely on the olfactory motive-response by which animals find and achieve harmonious, monogamous relationships. Thus, the second product was designed not to obscure the natural body odor but to cleverly assert it. And, in M.R. terms, an undeniable correspondence and natural attraction would result between appropriate compatible persons. It was called *Musk and Tallow.* An irritant jingle, in stereophonic sound, on the high-velocity repetition principle, was to be used: *"Don't Lie Fallow—Musk and Tallow!"* repeated many many times within a few seconds.

It was also decided that owing to the failure of *Downy,* it would be to certain advantage to make a clear break at this point and change the name of the mother company—a new name which would embrace both aspects of the M.R. postulate; and so it was decided: LADY APHRODITE.

Grand arranged that a number of prominent biologists, physicians, philosophers, church representatives, film stars, congresswomen, nursery-school teachers, and so on, should come forward in unsolicited endorsement of the moral correctness and practicality of the product.

Promotionwise, it did seem to capture the imagination of the public. Grand's contention at conference was that it appealed to the "magnificent bohemian strain in the great middle class," and "to the return-to-nature elements dormant within them like a sleeping giant."

"In offering these two products across this grand land of ours," he said at final conference, "Lady Aphrodite has presented a pure dichotomy. At last a satisfactory choice may be made, a side taken, and yet *each side* shall enjoy the security—on this particular issue at least—of *operating within an absolute.*

Gentlemen, I say this product may well spell 'home-run' in the hearts of Mr. and Mrs. U.S.A.!"

Small matter though, for both products were, as it turned out, nothing more nor less than some kind of delayed-action *stench-bomb*—hydrogen sulfide or the like—causing a great stench and embarrassment to a number of people. Apparently it was simply another joke by Grand at their expense, and not altogether in the best of taste. At least so the press thought (when they got wind of it) and they were down on this Grand and his staffers like the proverbial ton. It cost him plenty to clear.

VIII

"And how is our Miss Sally Hastings these days?"
Agnes asking this genially of Ginger Horton while
giving Guy a meaningfully coy glance—for she had
tried to interest her nephew in the young lady.

"Poor Sally," said Ginger Horton, putting on her
look of extremest nonchalance. "She's become rather
tiresome, I'm afraid."

"That *is* a shame," said Agnes. "Such a lovely girl
—didn't you think so, Guy?"

"A most charming girl," said Guy Grand.

"And yet, I must say, *you* didn't seem to notice,"

his aunt went on, rather severely, "hardly spoke two words all evening—though, if I've a shred of intuitiveness, she was very much attracted to *you*, Guy."

"We met later at her place," Guy explained.

"Guy, you didn't!" said Agnes in genuine annoyance.

"Yes, of course," said Guy. "Just for a little tête-à-tête—nothing more certainly."

"*Well*," said Agnes, taking a long sip of her tea, and pursing her lips before speaking again to Ginger, "that *is* a shame, Ginger. And such a *clever* girl, too; but then I suppose so many of them are, aren't they—young girls, I mean, of her sort? Personally, of course, I put *quality* before *cleverness*—don't *you*, Guy?"

"Oh, I should think that goes without saying," said Guy easily.

*

Grand's entrance into the world of championship boxing, significant though it may have been, went completely unnoticed by the savants of the press. They continued about their business, promoting the Champ. They said the Champ had plenty of heart and moxie, and that while he might not be the brightest guy in the whole world, by golly, he was nobody's fool, and pound for pound, he could punch with the best of them.

In the columns they set up hypothetical matches:

Maybe you're asking, "Could the Champ have taken the Rock's primeval right-cross?" The answer to that? He *could,* and he could have dished something out to boot! "*But,*" you want to know, "*could* he have handled the Bomber's Sunday-one, I mean the one that could snap a two-by-four from nine inches!" Look, you want me to tell you something? If Champy couldn't roll that punch, you know what he *could* do? He could just *laugh* it off! "Granted," you say, "but could the Champ have lasted with Big John L., when the chips were down bloody-bare-bone-kunckle in the 108th stanza?" You want my answer to that, buddy? Okay, I'll tell you something. I was standing with the Champ and his gray-haired Mom one Saturday afternoon on the corner of Darrow and Lex when some punk hood comes up and starts slapping Champ's Mom around.

"You dirty old slut!" he yelled, slapping her around. The Champ's Mom! Can you imagine!?! *Well,* if you think the American heavyweight boxing champion of the world stands idle while some cheap runt of a punk roughs up his *Mom—you've* got another think coming, Mister! *You'd* better put on your think-cap, Mister! The answer is *N . . . O . . .* spells "NO!" "Okay," you say, "so far, so hunky-do-ray-me, but could the Champ have notched Demetrias—when Demi was swinging with the old net and trident, and the Champ was hog-tied?" What? You want my answer to that buddy? Okay, just listen. If Champ . . .

The Champ was a national hero. He became a TV personality, and his stock in trade was a poignant, almost incredible, ignorance. He was good-natured and lovably stupid—and, boy-oh-boy, was he *tough!*

Well, Grand got through somehow, put his cards on the table (two million, tax-free) and made an arrangement whereby the Champ would throw the next fight in a gay or effeminate manner and, in fact, would behave that way all the time, on TV, in the ring, everywhere—swishing about, grimacing oddly, flinching when he struck a match, and so on.

The next big bout was due to go quite differently now. The challenger in this case was a thirty-three-year-old veteran of the ring named Texas Powell. Tex had an impressive record: 40 wins (25 by K.O.), 7 losses and 3 draws. He had been on the scene for quite a while and was known, or so the press insisted, as a "rugged customer," and a "tough cookie."

"Tex has got the punch," they said. "The big *if* is: Can he deliver it? Will he remain conscious long enough to deliver it? *There's* your Big If in tonight's Garden bout!"

Well, the fix was in with Tex too, of course—not simply to carry the fight, but to do so in the most flamboyantly homosexual manner possible. And finally, a fix—or *zinger,* as it was called in those days —was in with the Commission as well, a precaution taken under best advice as it turned out, because what happened in the ring that night was so "funny" that the bout might well have been halted at the opening bell.

Fortunately, what did happen didn't last too long. The Champ and the challenger capered out from their corners with a saucy mincing step, and, during the first cagey exchange—which on the part of each was like nothing so much as a young girl striking at a wasp with her left hand—uttered little cries of surprise and disdain. Then Texas Powell took the fight to the Champ, closed haughtily, and engaged him with a pesky windmill flurry which soon had the Champ covering up frantically, and finally shrieking, "I can't *stand* it!" before succumbing beneath the vicious peck and flurry, to lie in a sobbing tantrum on the canvas, striking his fists against the floor of the ring—more the bad loser than one would have expected. Tex tossed his head with smug feline contempt and allowed his hand to be raised in victory—while, at the touch, eyeing the ref in a questionable manner.

Apparently a number of people found the spectacle so abhorrent that they actually blacked-out.

IX

"Ginger . . ." Agnes began lightly, "when did you first realize that Sally Hastings was perhaps . . . well, a bit *common?*"

"Agnes, it was *Bitsy* who knew it first," exclaimed Ginger Horton with perfect candor.

"The dog?" asked Grand.

"What *can* you mean by that, Ginger?" Agnes wanted to know, dubious herself, yet casting her nephew a quick and cutting look to show where her allegiance lay even so.

"She didn't really love our Bitsy, Agnes," said Ginger narrowly, ". . . and Bitsy *couldn't* have cared less I assure you!"

*

Grand's work in cinema management and film editing had apparently not diminished his strong feeling for dramatic theatre, so that with the cultural ascension of television drama, he was all the more keen to get, as he put it, *"back on the boards."*

"There's no biz like show biz," he liked to quip to the other troupers, ". . . oh, we have our ups and downs, heck yes—but I wouldn't trade one whiff of grease paint on opening night, by gosh, for all the darn châteaux of France!"

Thus did he enter the field, not nominally of course, but in effect. There was at this time a rather successful drama hour on Sunday evening. "Our Town Playhouse" it was called and was devoted to serious fare; at least the viewers were told it was serious fare—truth to tell though, it was by any civilized standard, the crassest sort of sham, cant, and weak-kneed pornography imaginable. Grand set about to interfere with it.

His arrival was fairly propitious; the production in dress rehearsal at that moment was called *All Our Yesterdays*, a drama which, according to the sponsors, was to be, concerning certain emotions and viewpoints, more or less *definitive*.

Beginning with this production, Grand made it a point that he or his representative contact the hero or heroine of each play, while it was still in rehearsal, and reach some sort of understanding about final production. A million was generally sufficient.

The arrangement between Grand and the leading actress of *All Our Yesterdays* was simplicity itself. During final production, that is to say, the Sunday-night nation-wide presentation of the play, and at the top of her big end-of-the-second-act scene, the heroine suddenly turned away from the other players, approached the camera, and addressed the viewers, point-blank:

"Anyone who would allow this slobbering pomp and drivel in his home has less sense and taste than the beasts of the field!"

Then she pranced off the set.

Half the remaining actors turned to stare after her in amazement, while the others sat frozen in their last attitudes. There was a frenzy of muffled whispers coming from off-stage:

"What the hell!"

"Cue! Cue!"

"Fade it! For Christ's sake, fade it!"

Then there was a bit of commotion before it was

81

actually faded—one of the supporting actors had been trained in Russian methods and thought he could improvise the rest of the play, about twelve minutes, so there were one or two odd lines spoken by him in this attempt before the scene jerkily faded to blackness. A short documentary film about tarpon fishing was put on to fill out the balance of the hour.

The only explanation was that the actress had been struck by insanity; but even so, front-office temper ran high.

On the following Sunday, the production, *Tomorrow's Light,* took an unexpected turn while the leading actor, in the role of an amiable old physician, was in the midst of an emergency operation. His brow was knit in concern and high purpose, as the young nurse opposite watched his face intently for a sign.

"Dr. Lawrence," she said, "do you . . . do you think you can save Dr. Chester's son?"

Without relaxing his features, the doctor smiled, a bit grimly it seemed, before raising his serious brown eyes to her own.

"I'm afraid it isn't a question of saving *him,* Miss Nurse—I only wish it were—it's a question of saving my dinner."

The nurse evidenced a questioning look, just concealing the panic beneath it (*for he had missed his cue!*), so, laying aside his instruments, he continued, as in explanation:

"Yes, you see, I really think if I speak one more line of this drivel I'll lose my dinner." He nodded gravely at the table, ". . . vomit right into that incision I've made." He slowly drew off his rubber gloves, regarding the astonished nurse as he did so with mild indignation.

"Perhaps that would be *your* idea of a pleasant Sunday evening, Miss Nurse," he said reproachfully. "Sorry, it *isn't* mine!" And he turned and strode off the set.

The third time something like this happened, the producer and sponsor were very nearly out of their minds. Of course they suspected that a rival company was tampering with the productions, bribing the actors and so on. Security measures were taken. Directors were fired right and left. Rehearsals were held behind locked doors, and there was an attempt to keep the actors under constant surveillance, but . . . Grand always seemed to get in there somehow, with the old convincer.

In the aftermath, some of the actors paid the breach-of-contract fine of twenty-five or fifty thousand; others pleaded temporary insanity; still others gained a lot of publicity by taking a philosophic stand, saying that it was true, they had been overcome with nausea at that drivel, and that they themselves were too sensitive and serious for it, had too much integrity, moral fiber, etc. With a million behind them, none seemed to lack adequate defense arrangements. Those who were kicked out of their union usually became producers.

Meanwhile the show went on. People started tuning in to see what new outrage would happen; it even appeared to have a sort of elusive comic appeal. It became the talk of the industry; the rating soared— but somehow it looked bad. Finally the producer and the sponsor of the show were put on the carpet before Mr. Harlan, the tall and distinguished head of the network.

"Listen," he said to the sponsor as he paced the office, "we want your business, Mr. Levet, don't get me wrong—but if you guys can't control that show of yours . . . well, I mean *goddamn* it, what's going on over there?" He turned to the producer now, who was a personal friend of his: "For Christ's sake, Max, can't you get together a *show*, and put it on the way it's supposed to be without any somersaults? . . . is *that* so hard to do? . . . I mean *we* can't have this sort of thing going on, *you* know that, Max, we *simply cannot have* . . ."

"Listen, Al," said the producer, a short fat man who rose up and down on his toes, smiling, as he spoke, "we got the highest Trendex in the books right now."

"Max, goddamn it, I'd have the FCC down on my neck in another week—*you* can't schedule one kind of hour—have something go haywire every time and fill out with something else . . . I mean what the *hell* you got over there . . . *two* shows or *one,* for Christ's sake!"

"We got the top Trendex in the biz, Al."

"There are some goddamn things that are against the law, Max, and that kind of stuff you had going out last week, that '*I pity the moron whose life is so empty he would look at this,*' and that kind of crap *cannot go out over the air!* Don't you understand that? It's not *me,* Max, you know that. I wouldn't give a goddamn if you had a . . . a *mule* up there throwing it to some hot broad, I only wish we could, for Christ's sake—but there *is a question of lawful procedure* and . . ."

"How about if it's 'healthy satire of the media,' Al?"

". . . and—*what?*"

"We got the top of the book, Al."

"Wait a minute . . ."

"We got it, Al."

"Wait a minute, Max, I'm thinking, for Christ's sake . . . 'healthy satire of the media' . . . *It's* an angle, *it's* an angle. Jones might buy it . . . Jones at the FCC . . . if I could get to him first . . . he's stupid enough to buy it. Okay, it's an angle, Max—that's all I can say right now . . . it's an angle."

The critics for the most part, after lambasting the first couple of shows as "terrific boners," sat tight for a while, just to see which way the wind was going to blow, so to speak—then, with the rating at sky-rocket level, they began to suggest that the show might be worth a peek.

"An off-beat sleeper," one of them said, "don't miss it."

"*New* comedy," said a second, "a sophisticated take-off on the sentimental."

And another: "Here's humor at its highest."

Almost all agreed in the end that it was healthy satire.

After interfering with six or seven shows, Grand grew restive.

"I'm pulling out," he said to himself, "it may have been good money after bad all along."

It was just as well perhaps, because at the point when the producer and sponsor became aware of what was responsible for their vast audience, they began consciously trying to choose and shape each drama towards that moment of anomaly which had made the show famous. And somehow this seemed to spoil it. At any rate it very soon degenerated—back to the same old tripe. And of course it was soon back to the old rating as well—which, as in the early, pre-Grand days, was all right, but nothing, really, to be too proud of.

X

"Would you like to know why I remember that young Laird K. Russell so vividly, Agnes?" Esther was asking.

Ginger Horton sniffed to show unqualified disinterest and murmured something to her sleeping Bitsy.

"Esther, you can't be serious," said Agnes, turning to the others with a brilliant smile. "More tea, anyone?"

"I most certainly *would* like to know," said **Grand,** actually coming forward a little on his chair.

"Well," said Esther, "it was because he looked like my father."

"Esther, really!" cried Agnes.

"I mean *our* father, of course," Esther amended. "Yes, Agnes, he looked just like the photographs of Poppa as a young man. It struck me then, but I didn't realize it at the time. So perhaps it's not Laird K. Russell I'm remembering, you see, even now, but those photographs. You didn't know him, of course, Guy—he was a truly remarkable man."

"Young Russell do you mean, or Poppa?" asked Guy.

"Why Poppa, of course—surely you don't know Laird K. Russell?"

"Esther, in the name of heaven!" cried Agnes. "He's probably *dead* by now! How *can* you go on so about the man? Sometimes I wonder if you aren't trying quite deliberately to *upset* me. . . ."

*

Speaking of upsets though, Grand upset the equilibrium of a rather smart Madison Avenue advertising agency, Jonathan Reynolds, Ltd., by secretly buying it—*en passant,* so to speak—and putting in as president a pygmy.

At that time it was rare for a man of this skin-pigmentation or stature (much the less both) to hold down a top-power post in one of these swank agencies, and these two handicaps would have been difficult to overcome—though perhaps could have been overcome in due time had the chap shown a reasonable amount of savoir-faire and general ability, or the promise of developing it. In this case, however, Grand had apparently paid the man to behave in an eccentric manner—to scurry about the offices like a squirrel and to chatter raucously in his native tongue. It was more than a nuisance.

An account executive, for example, might be entertaining an extremely important client in his own office, a little tête-à-tête of the very first seriousness—perhaps with an emissary of one of the soap-flake kings—when the door would burst open and in would fly the president, scrambling across the room and under the desk, shrieking pure gibberish, and then out he'd go again, scuttling crabwise over the carpet, teeth and eyes blazing.

"What in God's name was that?" the client would ask, looking slowly about, his face pocked with a terrible frown.

"Why, that . . . that . . ." But the a.e. could not bring himself to tell, not after the first few times anyway. Evidently it was a matter of pride.

Later this a.e. might run into one of his friends

from another agency, and the friend would greet him:

"Say, hear you've got a new number one over at J.R., Tommy—what's the chap like?"

"Well, as a matter of fact, Bert . . ."

"You don't mean the old boy's got you on the *mat* already, Tommy. Ha-ha. *That* what you're trying to say?"

"No, Bert, it's . . . well I don't know, Bert, I *just don't know.*"

It was a matter of pride, of course. As against it, salaries had been given a fairly stiff boost, *and* titles. If these dapper execs were to go to another agency now, it would be at a considerable loss of dollars and cents. Most of the old-timers—and the younger ones too, actually—had what it took to stick it out there at J.R.

XI

"These sweet fluffs *are* good," said Ginger Horton, daintily taking what was perhaps her ninth cream puff from a great silver tray at hand, and giving Guy Grand a most coquettish look.

"Takes one to know one," said Guy, beaming and rolling his eyes.

Esther twittered, and Agnes looked extremely pleased.

*

Grand made quite a splash in the fall of '58 when he entered the "big-car" field with his sports line of Black Devil Rockets, a gigantic convertible. There were four models of the Rocket, each with a different fanciful name, though, except for the color of the upholstery, all four cars were identical. The big convertible was scaled in the proportions of an ordinary automobile, but was tremendous in size—was, in fact, *longer and wider than the largest Greyhound Bus in operation.*

"THERE'S POWER TO SPARE UNDER THIS BIG BABY'S FORTY-FOOT HOOD!" was a sales claim that gained attention.

Fronting the glittering crystal dash were two "racing-cup" seats with a distance of ten feet between them, and the big "gang's-all-here" seat in back would accommodate twelve varsity crewmen abreast in roomy comfort.

"Buy Yourself One *Whale* of a Car, Buddy!" read the giant ads. "From Stem to Stern She's a Flat One Hundred Feet! Ladylike Lines on a He-Man Hunk of Car!"

Performance figures were generally side-stepped, but a number of three-color billboards and full-page ads were headed: *"Performance?* Ask the Fella Behind the Wheel!" and featured, in apparently authentic testimonial, one of the Indianapolis speed kings

behind the wheel of the mammoth convertible. A
larger than average man, he was incredibly dwarfed
by the immense dimensions of the car. His tiny face,
just visible at the top of the wheel, was split in a grin
of insanity, like a toothpaste ad, a madman's laugh
frozen at the nightmare peak of hilarity, and it was
captioned:

*"Getting the feel of this big baby has been one real
thrill, believe you me!"*

The four identical models were shown at a display
room on Fifth Avenue, and though considered beyond the price range of most, were evidently sold.
At any rate, on the last day of the exposition they
were driven away, out and into the streets of mid-
town Manhattan during the five o'clock rush.

Despite their roominess, power, and road-holding
potential, the big cars did prove impractical in the
city, because their turning-arc—for the ordinary 90°
change of direction—was greater than the distance
between the street-angled buildings, so that by five
thirty all four of the sleek Devil Rockets were
wedged at angles across various intersections around
Columbus Circle, each a barrier to thoroughfare in
four directions, and causing quite a snarl indeed
until cranes and derricks could be brought up from
the East River to pry the big cars out.

New York authorities were quick to respond to the

flood of protests and got out an injunction to prevent Black Devil Rocket Corp. from further production.

"Personally," said one high-ranking city official, in an off-the-record remark in defense of the court's ruling—which was, after all, a flagrant infringement on the rights of free enterprise—". . . *personally* I frankly think the car is an ugly car and a . . . a *pretentious* car, and, as experience has shown us, it is an impractical car. I'll bet it's plenty expensive to run, too."

At last account though, Grand—himself fairly well in the background—was carrying on, pressing his fight to get the go-ahead and swing into full production with the big baby.

XII

"You *must* stay to dinner, Ginger," said Agnes. "And there *might* be a nice bit of fillet for our Bitsy," she added knowingly. "Do let me tell Cook you will!"

"But, my dear, we simply couldn't," said Ginger, casting a look flushed with girlish pride down at her own great scanty costume. "What about your nigras?"

"Cook and kitchen staff?" said Agnes, genuinely surprised. "Why, Ginger, really! But what's your feeling on it, Guy?"

"Sorry, don't follow," said Guy.

"Well, Ginger seems to think that our servers might be . . . might be . . ."

"Might be sent straight off their rockers with bestial desire, you mean?" asked Grand tersely. "Hmm —Ginger may be right. Better safe than sorry in these matters I've always said."

*

Guy liked playing the fool, it's true—though some say there was more to his antics than met the eye. At any rate, one amusing diversion in which he took a central role himself was when he played *grand gourmet* at the world's most luxurious restaurants.

Guy would arrive in faultless evening attire, attended by his poker-faced valet, who carried a special gourmet's chair and a large valise of additional equipment. The chair, heavily weighted at the bottom so it could not be easily overturned, was also fitted with a big waist strap which was firmly secured around Grand's middle as soon as he was seated. Then the valet would take from the valise a huge rubber bib and attach it to Guy while the latter surveyed the menu in avid conference with a bevy of hosts—the maître d', the senior waiter, the wine steward, and at least one member of the chef's staff.

Guy Grand was the last of the big spenders and, as

such, a great favorite at these restaurants; due to his eccentric behavior during the meal however, the management always took care to place him at a table as decentralized as possible—on the edge of the terrace, in a softly lit alcove, or, preferably, at a table entirely obscured by a canopy arrangement which many restaurants, after his first visit, saw fit to have on hand for Guy's return.

Following the lengthy discussion to determine the various courses, the waist strap was checked, and Guy would sit back in his chair, rubbing his hands together in sophisticated anticipation of the taste treats to come.

When the first course did arrive, an extraordinary spectacle would occur. At the food's very aroma, Grand, still sitting well back from the table, as in fanatical self-restraint, would begin to writhe ecstatically in his chair, eyes rolling, head lolling, saliva streaming over his ruddy jowls. Then he would suddenly stiffen, his face a mask of quivering urgency, before shouting: "*Au table!*" whereupon he would lurch forward, both arms cupped out across the table, and wildly scoop the food, dishes and all, towards his open mouth. Following this fantastic clatter and commotion—which left him covered from the top of his head to his waist with food—the expressionless valet would lean forward and unfasten the chair strap, and Guy would bolt from the table and rush pell-mell towards the kitchen, covered and dripping with food, hair matted with it, one arm extended full length as in a congratulatory handshake, shouting at the top of his voice:

"MES COMPLIMENTS AU CHEF!"

Upon his return to the table, he would be strapped into the chair again, hosed-down by a little water pump from the valet's case, and dried with a big towel; then the performance would be repeated with each course.

Restaurants who used a special canopy to conceal Grand from the other diners did so at considerable risk, because at the moment of completing each course he would bolt for the kitchen so quickly that, unless the waiters were extremely alert and dexterous in pulling aside the canopy, he would bring the thing down on his head and, like a man in a collapsed tent, would flail about inside it, upsetting the table, and adding to the general disturbance, or worse, as sometimes did happen, he might regain his feet within the canopy and career blindly through the plush restaurant, toppling diners everywhere, and spreading the disturbance—and, of course, if he ever reached the kitchen while still inside the canopy, it could be actually calamitous.

The open-mouthed astonishment of waiters, diners

and others who were witness to these scenes was hardly lessened by the bits of bland dialogue they might overhear between the maître d', who was also in on the gag, and the valet.

"Chef's *Béarnaise* pleased him," the maître d' would remark soberly to the valet, "I could tell."

The valet would agree with a judicious nod, as he watched Grand storming through the restaurant. "He's awful keen tonight."

"In the *Béarnaise*," the maître d' would suddenly confide in an excited whisper, "the peppercorns were *bruised* merely by dropping them!" And the two men would exchange dark knowing glances at this revelation.

By the last course Grand would be utterly exhausted, and the exquisite dessert would invariably prove too much for his overtaxed senses. At the first taste of it, he would go into a final tantrum and then simply black out. He always had to be carried from the restaurant on a stretcher, leaving waiters and diners staring agape, while the maître d' stood respectfully by the door with several of his staff.

"Boy, was that guy ever *nuts!* Huh?" a wide-eyed young waiter would exclaim as he stood with the maître d', gazing after the departing figures. But the latter would appear not to have heard.

"The last of the *grand gourmets*," he would sigh,

and there was always a trace of wistful nostalgia in his face when he turned back from the door. "No, sir, they don't make taste buds like *that* any more."

Connivance with the maître d's of these top restaurants was an expensive affair, and there was a shake-up in more than one veteran staff due to it. Those who lost their jobs though were usually in a position to open fairly smart restaurants of their own —assuming, of course, they didn't care to buy the one from which they were fired.

XIII

"In *literature,* of course," Ginger Horton was saying, "the *best* writing comes out of the *heart,* and *not* the *head!*"

"*I'll* buy that!" agreed Guy Grand, coming forward on his big chair in ready interest, his voice going a bit taut with feeling as he continued:

"For *my* money the best . . . the *very best* darn writing is done right out of the old guts, by God!" And he gave his budding paunch a short slap to strengthen his meaning.

"Good Heavens," said Esther crouching forward into a sea of giggles.

"And *no rewrite!*" said Guy strongly, ". . . right out of the old guts onto the goddamn paper!"

"Guy!" exclaimed Agnes, "really!" It was well known that Ginger Horton *did* write—wrote unceasingly—relentless torrents of a deeply introspective prose.

"Sorry," muttered Grand, sitting back again, "get a bit carried away sometimes, I expect."

"*Feeling and passion!*" agreed Ginger Horton in a shriek. "Of course most of the nasty little people around don't feel a *thing! Not a single thing!*"

"Interesting you should bring that up," said Guy, reaching in his coat pocket and withdrawing a small memo-book, which he thumbed through as he continued:

"Fellow I met on the train—I won't mention his name if you don't mind, because the thing is still pretty much on the drawing board, so to speak . . . but I can tell you *this:* he's one of the top-brass along 'Publishers' Row'—well, we got to talking, one thing and another, and he offered to let me in on a new scheme of his. How sound it is I *don't* know, but he's willing to let me in on the ground floor—at *second-story prices,* of course—" added Guy with a good-natured chuckle. "And *there's* your old six-and-seven again, but, still and all, that's to be expected in the investment game. Well, his scheme—and I'd like to put out a feeler on it—is to issue a series of Do-It-Yourself Portables . . . the *Do-It-Yourself Shakespeare,* the *D.H. Do-It-Yourself Lawrence,* and so on."

"What on earth—" Ginger began crossly.

"*His* idea," said Guy, "—and I don't pretend to know how sound it is—is to issue the regular texts of well-known works, with certain words, images, bits of dialogue, and what have you, left *blank* . . . just spaces there, you see . . . which *the reader fills in.*"

"Well, I never—" said Ginger irately.

"Oh yes, here we are," said Grand, evidently finding the place he was looking for in the memo-book, "Yes, now here's some of his promotional copy . . . rough draft, mind you . . . let's see, yes, this is for Kafka's *Do-It-Yourself Trial.* Goes like this:

'Now you too can experience that same marvelous torment of ambiguity and haunting glimpse of eternal beauty which tore this strange artist's soul apart and stalked him to his very grave! Complete with optional imagery selector, master word table and *writer's-special* ball-point pen, thirty-five cents.' "

Ginger Horton made a gurgling sound of anger preparatory to speaking, but Guy was quick to press on:

"And here we are for the *Look Homeward* (*Your-self*) *Angel:*

'Hey there, reader-writer—how would you like to spew your entrails right out onto a priceless Sarouk carpet?!? Huh? Right in the middle of somebody's living room with everyone watching? Huh? Well, by golly, you *can*, etcetera, etcetera.'

"As I say, it's rough-draft copy, of course—needs tightening up, brightening up—but what's your feeling on it, Ginger? Think it might spell 'blast-off' in the hearts of Mr. and Mrs. Front Porch?"

"What? Well I wouldn't put a . . . a *single cent* into it!" said Ginger with considerable emphasis.

"Oh it's just too dreadful, Guy," exclaimed Agnes. "You mustn't."

"Hmm. I suppose you're right," said Guy, ". . . hard to say really. *Might* catch on—might not . . . just wanted to put out a feeler or two on it. Always best to keep an open mind in the investment game."

*

Grand had a bit of fun when he engaged a man to smash crackers with a sledge-hammer in Times Square.

The stout fellow arrived with his gear—a box of

saltine crackers and a sixty-pound sledge—at precisely 9 A.M. and "set up shop," as Guy expressed it, just outside the subway entrance on Forty-Second Street, the busiest thoroughfare in the world at this particular hour.

Dressed in khaki and wearing a tin hat, the curious man forged his way through the deluge of people pouring out of the subway, and then in the very midst of the surging throng, opened the brass-studded pouch attached to his belt, extracted a single saltine cracker, and stooped over to place it carefully on the sidewalk.

"Watch yourself!" he shouted as he stood up, gesturing impatiently. "Keep clear! Mind your step!" And then, raising the hammer to shoulder height, he brought it down in one horrendous blow on the cracker—not only smashing it to dust, but also producing several rather large cracks in the sidewalk.

Within a few minutes the area was swollen with onlookers—all but the nearest of whom had to crane their heads wildly or leap up and down to get a glimpse of the man in the tin hat now as he squatted to examine the almost invisible dust of the cracker. "Sure mashed it, didn't it?" he muttered, as to himself, in a professional manner.

"What'd he say?" demanded several people urgently of those near the operation.

"Said it 'sure *mashed* it,'" someone explained.

"'*Mashed* it'?" snorted another. "Boy, you can say *that* again!"

Guy Grand was on the scene as well, observing the diverse comments and sometimes joining in.

"Hey, how come you doin' that?" he asked directly of the man in the tin hat.

The man laid out another cracker, placing it with great care.

"This?" he said, standing and raising the big sledge. "Oh, this is all technical."

"What's he say?"

"Says it's technical."

"*What?*"

"*Technical.*"

"Yeah, well, what's that he's hitting with the hammer? What is that? It looks like a *cracker*."

"Naw, what'd he hit a *cracker* for—you kiddin'?"

"Boy, look how that sledge busts up the sidewalk! Man, that's some *sledge* he's got there!"

Within a very short time indeed, the gathering had spilled over into the street, interfering with the traffic there and causing the tough Forty-Second Street cop to wade growling into the heart of the crowd. "Okay, break it up!" he kept saying. "Shove off!" And when he reached the center where the operation was being carried out, he stood for a long while with his cap pushed back on his head, hands on hips, and a nasty frown on his face, as he watched the man in the tin hat smash a few more crackers with the giant sledge.

"Are you workin' for the *city*, bud?" he finally asked in an irate voice.

"That's right," said the tin-hat man without looking up. "City planning. This is technical."

"Yeah," said the cop, "well, you sure picked a hell of a place to do it, that's all I got to say." Then, adjusting his cap, he started pushing at the crowd.

"Okay, let's keep movin'!" he shouted. "Break it up here! Get on to work! This is technical—*shove off!*"

Diversion is at a premium at this hour however, and the crowd was not to be dispersed so easily. After a while the hoses had to be brought. When the ruse was discovered, Grand had a spot of bother clearing it.

XIV

"Perhaps Ginger could slip into one of your things," suggested Guy.

Esther childlishly covered her mouth to hide a laugh, and darted glances of mischief and glee at the others, while Agnes drew in her breath before speaking:

"I'm afraid we do *not* take the same size, Guy!"

Agnes, thin as a whip, was perhaps a size nine; Ginger's great size must have been well into the sixties.

Ginger, too, shook her head emphatically.

"Charles would simply die if I wore a frock he hadn't done!" she said.

"Has Charles done any chemises for you?" Guy inquired.

"I *wanted* Charles to do some little Roman chemises for me, Guy," Ginger confided. "I think I have the fullness for them—well, it would have meant giving up all my little feminine frills and laces, of course, and Charles simply would not hear of it! He said it would be a perfect *crime*—and he does so love to work with his laces, Guy, I simply didn't have the heart! But then what's your feeling on it, Guy?" she asked finally, giving a Carmenesque toss of her head.

"Charles *could* be right, of course," said Guy, after allowing it a moment's thought.

*

Grand gave a bit of a shock to the British white-hunters along the Congo (as well as to a couple of venerable old American writers who were there on safari at the time) when he turned up in a major hunting expedition with a 75-millimeter howitzer.

"She throws a muzzle-velocity of twelve thousand f.p.s.," Grand liked to quip. "She'll stop anything on this continent."

Ordinarily used by the French Army as an artillery

fieldpiece, the big gun, stripped of all but its barrel, chamber, and firing mechanism, still weighed well over a hundred and fifty pounds.

"She'll stop anything that moves," Guy would say, "—including a surfaced *whale*."

Grand had three natives carry the giant gun, while he, wearing a huge cushion-device around his stomach and a pith helmet so enormous that half his face was concealed beneath it, sauntered jauntily alongside, speaking knowledgeably to other members of the party about every aspect of firearms and big-game hunting.

"A spot of bother in Kenya bush the other day," he would say, " the big cat took two of our best boys." Then he would give his monstrous weapon an affectionate pat and add knowingly, "—the cat changed her tune when she'd had a taste of the old seventy-five! Yessir, this baby carries a real *wallop,* you can bet your life on that!"

About once an hour, Grand would stop and dramatically raise his hand, bringing the entire safari to a halt, while he and one of his trusty natives (heretofore known as the "best guide in Central Africa") would sniff the air, nostrils flared and quivering, eyes a bit wild.

"There's cat in the bush," Guy would say tersely, and while the rest of the party looked on in pure

amazement, Grand, big helmet completely obscuring his sight, would take up the huge gun and, staggering under its weight, brace it against the great cushion at his stomach, and blindly fire one of the mammoth shells into the bush, blasting a wide swath through the tall grass and felling trees as though they were stalks of corn. The recoil of the weapon would fling Grand about forty feet backwards through the air where he would land in a heap, apparently unconscious.

"The baby packs a man-sized recoil," Guy would say later. "The Mannlicher, of course, is nothing more than a *toy*."

Due to the extreme noise produced by the discharge of the 75, any actual game in the area was several miles away by the time the reverberations were stilled—so that these safaris would often go from start to finish without ever firing a shot, other than the occasional big boom from Grand's 75.

African hunting expeditions are serious and expensive affairs, and this kind of tomfoolery cost Grand a pretty penny. It did provide another amusing page for his memory book though—and the old native guides seemed to enjoy it as well.

XV

"Hold on, here's a bit of news," said Guy then, suddenly brightening in his big chair and smartly slapping the newspaper spread across his lap. The banner read:

PRESIDENT ASKS NATION FOR FAITH
IN GIANT SPACE PROGRAM
Jackass Payload Promised

He read it aloud in sonorous tones, but Ginger pooh-poohed the claim.

"Probably one of these teeny-weeny Mexican burros!" she cried. "Jackass indeed!" She was a notorious foe of the administration.

"I *wouldn't* underestimate our Mister Uncle Sambo if I were you," cautioned Guy, raising a rather arch look for Ginger and the others.

"Why those Mexican burros are no bigger than a minute!" Ginger insisted.

"Ginger's right," put in Agnes sharply, donning her spectacles—as she almost invariably did when taking political issue with Guy—to peer down at him then over the top of them, her face pinched and testy. "It would make a good deal more sense to send *that* great ninny up into space!" She flung back her head in a veritable cackle of delight at the idea. "I say blast that whole pack of ninnies right out into fartherest outer space!"

Grand laid his paper aside.

"I *don't* think I'm an intolerant person," he said quietly, but with considerable feeling, as he rose to his feet, "nor one of hasty opinion—but, in times like these, when the very *mettle* of this nation is in the crucible, I say that brand of talk is not far short of *damnable treason!*" Still glowering, he did a funny little two-step and ended in a smart salute. "I'm afraid I'll not be staying for dinner myself, by the way," he added matter-of-factly.

116

"Guy, I simply will *not* hear of it!" cried cross Agnes, snatching her glasses from her nose and fixing the man with a terrible frown. "Surely you *shall* stay!"

"Guy, Guy, Guy," keened Esther, wagging her dear gray head, "always on the go."

"Yes, only wish I *could* stay," agreed Guy sadly. "Best push on though—back to harness, back to grind."

*

It was along towards the end though that Grand achieved, in terms of public outrage, his *succès d'estime*, as some chose to call it, when he put out to sea in his big ship, the S.S. *Magic Christian* . . . the ship sometimes later referred to as "The Terrible Trick Ship of Captain Klaus." Actually it was the old *Griffin*, a passenger liner which Grand bought and had reconditioned for about fifty million.

A vessel of 30,000 tons, the *Christian* had formerly carried some eleven-hundred-odd passengers. Grand converted it into a one-class ship, outfitted to accommodate four hundred passengers, in a style and comfort perhaps unknown theretofore outside princely domains of the East. Each cabin on the *Christian* was a palace in miniature; the appointments were so lavish and so exquisitely detailed that they might better be imagined than described. All the cabins were of course above deck and outside, each with a twenty-foot picture window and French doors to a private patio commanding a magnificent expanse of sea and sky. There were fine deep rugs throughout each suite and period-furnishings of first account, private bars, chaise longues, log-burning fireplaces, king-sized beds (canopy optional), an adjoining library-den (with a set of the *Britannica* and the best in smart fiction), tape recorders, powder rooms, small Roman bath and steam cabinet. Walls were generally in a quiet tone of suede with certain paneling of teak and rosewood.

Ship's dining room was styled after Maxim's in Paris whose staff had been engaged to prepare the meals and to serve them with inconspicuous grace against a background of soft music provided by the Juilliard String Quartette. The balance of ship's appointments were in harmonious key—there was, for example, a veritable jewel box of a theatre, seating just four hundred, fashioned in replica of the one in the Monte Carlo Casino; and the versatile repertory group, Old Vic Players, were on stand-by for two shows a day.

Ship's doctor, aside from being an able physician, was also a top-flight mental specialist, so that Problem-Counseling was available to the passengers at all hours.

But perhaps the most carefully thought-out nicety of the *Christian* was its principal lounge, the Marine Room—a large room, deep below decks, its wall (that which was part of ship's hull) glassed so that the passengers sat looking out into the very heart of the sea. An ocean-floor effect was maintained by the regular release of deep-sea creatures from a water-line station near the bow, and through the use of powerful daylight kliegs there was afforded a breath-taking panorama—with giant octopi, huge rainbow-colored ray, serpents, great snowy angelfish, and fantastic schools of luminous tetra constantly gliding by or writhing in silent majestic combat a few feet from the relaxed passengers.

Though the *Magic Christian* received its share of prevoyage hullabaloo (*Life* magazine devoted an issue to photographs, enthusiastically captioned), its only form of paid advertisement was a simple announcement of its sailing date, which appeared in *The Times* and in the *National Geographic*. The fare was not mentioned (though *Life* had said it was "about five thousand") and the announcement was set in small heavy type, boxed with a very black border. "For the Gracious Few . . ." it opened, and went on to state in a brief, restrained apology, that *not everyone* could be accepted, that applications for passage on the *Christian* were necessarily carefully screened, and that those who were refused should not take offense. "Our criteria," it closed, "may *not* be yours."

Ship's quarters were not shown until the applicant had been accepted, and then were shown by appointment.

The ship was christened by the Queen of England.

All of this had a certain appeal and the applications poured in. More than a few people, in fact, were *demanding* passage on the *Christian's* first voyage. Those just back from holiday were suddenly planning to go abroad again; scores rushed home simply to qualify and make the trip. For many, the maiden voyage of the *Magic Christian* became a must.

Meanwhile Guy Grand, well in the background, was personally screening the applications according to some obscure criteria of his own, and apparently he had himself a few laughs in this connection. In the case of one application, for example, from a venerable scioness of Roman society, he simply scrawled moronically across it in blunt pencil: "Are *you* kidding?!? *No* wops!" The woman was said to have had a nervous breakdown and did later file for a million on defamation. It cost Grand a pretty to clear it.

On the other hand, he accepted—or rather, engaged—as passengers, a group from a fairly sordid freak show, most of whom could not be left untended, along with a few gypsies, Broadway types, and the like, of offensive appearance and doubtful character. These, however, were to be kept below decks for the first few days out, and, even so, numbered only about forty in all, so that a good nine-tenths of the passenger list, those on deck when the *Christian* set sail in such tasteful fanfare that Easter morn, were top-drawer gentry and no mistake.

Unique among features of the *Christian* was its video communication system from the bridge to other parts of the ship. Above the fireplace in each cabin was a small TV screen and this provided direct visual communication with the Captain at the wheel and with whatever other activity was going on there, giving as it did a view of almost the entire bridge. These sets could be switched *on* or *off*, but the first day they were left *on* before the passengers arrived, in order to spare anyone the embarrassment of not knowing what the new gimmick was. So that when passengers entered their cabins now they saw at once, there on the screen above the fireplace: the Captain at the wheel. Captain Klaus. And for this person, Guy Grand had engaged a professional actor, a distinguished silver-haired man whose every gesture inspired the deepest confidence. He wore a double row of service ribbons on his dark breast and deported himself in a manner both authoritative and pleasingly genial—as the passengers saw when he turned to face the screen, and this he did just as soon as they were all settled and under way.

He was filling his pipe when he turned to camera, but he paused from this to smile and touch his cap in easy salute.

"Cap'n Klaus," he said, introducing himself with warm informality, though certainly at no sacrifice to his considerable bearing. "Glad to have you aboard."

He casually picked up a pointer stick and indicated a chart on the nearby wall.

"Here's our course," he said, "nor' by nor'east, forty-seven degrees."

Then he went on to explain the mechanics and lay-out of the bridge, the weather and tide conditions at present, their prospects, and so on, using just enough technical jargon throughout all this to show that he knew what he was about. He said that the automatic-pilot would be used from time to time, but that he personally preferred handling the wheel himself, adding good-humoredly that in his opinion "a ship favored men to machines."

"It may be an old-fashioned notion," he said, with a wise twinkle, ". . . but to me, a ship is a woman."

At last he gave a final welcome-salute, saying again: "Glad to have you aboard," and turned back to his great wheel.

This contact with the bridge and the fatherly Captain seemed to give the passengers an added sense of participation and security; and, indeed, things couldn't have gone more smoothly for the first few hours.

It was in the very early morning that something untoward occurred, at about three A.M.—and of course almost everyone was asleep. They had watched their screens for a while: the Captain in the cozy bridge house, standing alone, pipe glowing, his strong eyes sweeping the black water ahead— then they had switched off their sets. There were a few people though who were still up and who had their sets on; and, of these few, there were perhaps three who happened to be watching the screen at a certain moment—when in the corner of the bridge house, near the door, there was a shadow, an odd movement . . . then suddenly the appearance of a sinister-looking person, who crept up behind the Captain, hit him on the head, and seized the wheel as the screen blacked out.

The people who had seen this were disturbed and, in fact, were soon rushing about, rousing others, wanting to go to the bridge and so on. And they did actually get up a party and went to the bridge—only to be met at the top of the ladder by the Captain himself, unruffled, glossing it over, blandly assuring them that nothing was wrong, nothing at all, just a minor occurrence. And, of course, back in the cabins, there he was on the screen again, Captain Klaus, steady at the helm.

Those three who had seen the outrage, being in such a hopeless minority, were thought to have been drunk or in some way out of their minds, and were gently referred to ship's doctor, the mental specialist, so the incident passed without too much notice.

And things went smoothly once more, until the next evening—when, in the exquisite gaming rooms just off the Marine Lounge, one of the roulette croupiers was seen, by several people, to be cheating . . . darting his eyes about in a furtive manner and then interfering with the bets, snatching them up and stuffing them in his pocket, that sort of thing.

It was such an unheard-of outrage that one old duke fainted dead away. The croupier was hustled out of the gaming room by Captain Klaus himself, who deplored the incident profusely and declared that the next dozen spins were on the house, losing bets to remain untouched for that time—gracious recompense, in the eyes of a sporting crowd, and applauded as such; still, the incident was not one easily forgotten.

Another curious thing occurred when some of the ladies went, individually, to visit the ship's doctor. For the most part they had simply dropped around to pick up a few aspirin, sea-sickness pills—or merely to have a reassuring chat with the amiable physician. Several of these ladies, however, were informed that they looked "rather queer" and that an examination might be in order.

"Better safe than sorry," the doctor said, and then, during the examination, he invariably seemed to discover what he termed "a latent abrasion"—on the waist, side, hip, or shoulder of the woman—and though the abrasion could not be seen, the doctor deemed it required a compress.

"Nothing serious," he explained, "still it's always wise to take precautions." And so saying he would apply a *huge compress* to the area, a sort of gigantic Band-Aid about a foot wide and several inches thick, with big adhesive flaps that went halfway around the body. The tremendous bulk of these compresses was a nuisance, causing as they did, great deforming bulges beneath the women's smart frocks. They were almost impossible to remove. One woman was seen running about with one on her head, like a big white hat.

First lifeboat drill was scheduled for the following morning. Shortly before it, Captain Klaus came on the screen and smilingly apologized for the inconvenience and gave a leisurely and pleasantly informative talk about the drill and its necessity.

"Better safe than sorry," he said in a genial close to his little talk.

When the drill signal sounded, they all got into life jackets—which were the latest thing and quite unlike standard passenger-ship equipment—and then, grumbling good-naturedly, they started for their boat stations; but an extraordinary thing happened: two minutes after they had put them on, the life jackets began inflating in a colossal way. Apparently the very act of donning the jacket set off some device which inflated it. The extraordinary thing was that each one blew up so big that it simply obscured the person wearing it, ballooning out about them, above their heads, below their feet, and to a diameter of perhaps twelve feet—so that if they were in an open space, such as their cabins, the lounge, or on deck, they simply rolled or lolled about on the floor, quite hidden from view, whereas if they were in a corridor, they were hopelessly stuck.

In any event, almost no one escaped the effects of the faulty life jacket; so it was—after they deflated —with a good deal of annoyance that they came back

126

to the cabins, quite ready to hear Captain Klaus' explanation of what had gone amiss.

Unfortunately though, the foghorn, which had been put to practice during the drill, was now evidently jammed. At any rate, it continued steadily during the Captain's after-drill talk and completely shut out his voice, so that it was like looking at someone talk behind several layers of glass. The Captain himself didn't seem to realize that he wasn't coming through, and he went on talking for quite a while, punctuating his remarks with various little facial gestures to indicate a whole gamut of fairly intense feelings about whatever it was he was saying.

The business with the foghorn was more serious than at first imagined; it continued, blasting without let-up, for the rest of the voyage.

Quite incidental to what was happening during the drill, fifty crew members took advantage of the occasion to go around to the cabins, lounges, and dining rooms, and to substitute a thin length of balsa wood for one leg of every chair, table, and dresser on ship.

When the Captain finished his lengthy and voiceless discourse, he smiled, gave an easy salute and left the bridge house. It was about this time that all the furniture began to collapse—in half an hour's time there wasn't one standing stick of it aboard the *Christian*.

Strange and unnatural persons began to appear—in the drawing rooms, salons, at the pool. During the afternoon tea dance, a gigantic *bearded-woman,* stark naked, rushed wildly about over the floor, interfering with the couples, and had to be forcibly removed by ship's doctor.

The plumbing went bad, too; and finally one of the *Christian's* big stacks toppled—in such a way as to give directly on to ship's dining room, sending oily smoke billowing through. And, in fact, from about this point on, the voyage was a veritable nightmare.

Large curious posters were to be seen in various parts of the ship:

SUPPORT MENTAL HEALTH

LET'S KEEP THE CLAP OUT
OF CHAPPAQUIDDICK

as well as rude slogans, vaguely political, scrawled in huge misshapen letters across walls and decks alike:

DEATH TO RICH!
BLOW UP U.S.!

Due to the strain of untoward events, more than one passenger sought solace and reassurance from the problem-counselor, the ship's distinguished doctor.

"Doctor, what *in the name of God* is going on here!" the frenzied passenger would demand.

The doctor would answer with a quizzical smile, arching his brows, only mildly censorious. "Fairweather sailor?" he would gently chide, ". . . hmm? Cross and irritable the moment things aren't going exactly to suit you? Now just what seems to be the trouble?"

" *'Trouble'!?!*" exclaimed the outraged passenger. "Good Lord, Doctor, surely you don't think my complaint is an . . . an unreasonable one?"

The doctor would turn his gaze out to sea, thin fingers pressed beneath his chin in a delicate pyramid of contemplation, wistfully abstract for a moment before turning back to address the patient frankly.

"Deep-rooted and unreasonable fears," he would begin in a grand, rich voice, "are most often behind our anxieties . . ." and he would continue in this vein until the passenger fairly exploded with impatience.

"Great Scott, Doctor! I didn't come here for a lecture on *psychology*—I came to find out what *in the name of Heaven* is going on *aboard this ship!*"

In the face of these outbursts however, the doctor almost invariably retained his calm, regarding the patient coolly, searchingly, making a few careful notes on his pad.

"Now, you say that 'the life jacket *over inflated*,' and that you were 'stuck in the corridor'—that was your expression, I believe, '*stuck in the corridor*'— and at that moment you felt a certain *malaise*, so to speak. Now, let me ask you *this* . . ." Or again, on other occasions, he might behave eccentrically, his head craned far to one side, regarding the patient out of the corners of his eyes, a sly, mad smile on his lips which moved in an inaudible whisper, almost a hiss.

Finally, the patient, at the end of his tether, would leap to his feet.

"Well, in the name of God, Doctor, the least you can do is let me have some *tranquillizers!*"

But the doctor, as it turned out, was not one given to prescribing drugs promiscuously.

"Escape into drugs?" he would ask, wagging his head slowly. "Mask our fears in an artificial fog?" And there was always a trace of sadness in his smile, as he continued, "No, I'm afraid the trouble is *in ourselves*, you see." Then he would settle back expansively and speak with benign countenance. "Running away from problems is scarcely the solution to them. I *believe* you'll thank me in years to come." And at last he would lean forward in quiet confidence. "Do you mind if I ask you a few questions about your . . . your *early childhood?*"

When Captain Klaus next appeared on the screen, he looked as though he had been sleeping in two feet of water. Completely disheveled, his ribbons dangling in unsightly strands, his open coat flapping, his unknotted tie strung loosely around his collar, he seemed somewhat drunk as well. With a rude wave of his hand he dismissed bridge personnel and lurched toward the video screen, actually crashing into it, and remaining so close that his image was all distorted.

"We'll get the old tub through!" he was shouting at deafening volume, and at that moment he was attacked from behind by a ruffian type who was carrying a huge hypodermic and appeared to over-power the Captain and inject something into the top of his head, then to seize the wheel, wrenching it violently, before the screen went black.

Also, it was learned about this time that because of fantastic miscalculation on the part of the ship's-stores officer, the only food left aboard now was potatoes.

Thus did the *Christian* roar over the sea, through fair weather and foul.

Guy Grand was aboard of course, as a passenger, complaining bitterly, and in fact kept leading assault parties in an effort to find out, as he put it, "What the devil's going on on the bridge!"

But they were always driven back by a number of odd-looking men with guns and knives near the ladder.

"Who the deuce are those chaps?" Grand would demand as he and the others beat a hasty retreat along the deck. "I don't like the looks of this!"

Occasionally the communications screen in each of the cabins would light up to reveal momentarily what was taking place on the bridge, and it was fairly incredible. The bridge house itself now was a swaying rubble heap and the Captain was seen intermittently, struggling with various assailants, and finally with what actually appeared to be a gorilla—the beast at last overpowering him and flinging him bodily out of the bridge house and, or so it seemed, into the sea itself, before seizing the wheel, which he seemed then to be trying to tear from its hub.

It was about this time that the ship, which, as it developed, had turned completely around in the middle of the ocean, came back into New York harbor under full steam, and with horns and whistles screaming, ploughed headlong into the big Forty-Seventh Street pier.

Fortunately no one was injured on the cruise; but, even so, it went far from easy with Grand—he had already sunk plenty into the project, and just how much it cost him to keep clear in the end, is practically anyone's guess.

XVI

"To speak seriously though," said Guy Grand, *"does* anyone have news of Bill Thorndike? I haven't had a word in the longest."

Ginger Horton set her cup down abruptly.

"That . . . that damn *nut!*" she said. *"No* and I *couldn't* care less!"

"Who?" asked Esther.

"Dr. Thorndike," explained Agnes, "that extraordinary dentist whom Ginger went to—he and Guy were friends at school together; isn't that right, Guy?"

"Yes, quite good friends too," said Guy. "Poor fellow, had a nervous breakdown or something from what Ginger says. No, I haven't had a word from him in the longest. How was he then, when you last saw him, Ginger?"

Grand had made this inquiry any number of times, and then had always glossed over Ginger's account of the incident, as though he could not fully take it in.

"The *last time!*" she cried. "Why I only saw him once, of course—on *your* recommendation—and once too often it was too! Good God, don't tell me you've forgotten *that* again? Why he was absolutely insane! He said to me, 'These molars are soft, Mrs. Horton!' or some such ridiculous thing. 'We'd better get you onto a soft-food regime right away!' he said, and then, without another word about it, while I was still leaning back with my mouth open, he dropped a *raw egg* into my mouth and rushed out of the room, waving his arms and yelling at the top of his voice. Raving mad!"

"Hmm—not like Bill Thorndike," said Grand. "First-rate dentist, he used to be. You never went back to him then?"

"I *certainly did not!* I went straight to the nearest police station, that's where I went! And reported him!"

Grand frowned a look of mild disapproval.

"I'm afraid that won't help Bill's standing with the Association any."

"Well, I should hope *not!*" said Ginger Horton as strongly as she could.

"How Uncle Edward used to love raw eggs!" said Esther. "Do you remember, Agnes?"

"It's hardly the same thing, Esther," said Agnes.

"Well, he always had them with a sort of sauce," Esther recalled. "Worcestershire sauce, I suppose it was."

"It could have been some new form of deficiency treatment, of course, Ginger," Agnes said. "I mean if your molars *were* soft . . ." But in the face of Ginger Horton's mounting exasperation, she broke off and turned to Guy, "What do you think, Guy?"

"Bill always *was* up-to-the-minute," Guy agreed. "Always onto the latest. Very progressive in school affairs, that sort of thing—oh nothing disreputable of course—but, I mean to say, as far as being onto the latest in . . . dentistry techniques, well I'm certainly confident that Bill—"

"He just plopped that raw egg right into my mouth!" said Ginger shrilly. "Why I didn't even know what it was! And that isn't all—the instruments, and *everything* else there were crazy! There was some kind of wooden paddle . . ."

"Spatula?" prompted Guy helpfully.

"No, *not* a spatula! Good Heavens! A big wooden oar, about four feet long, actually leaning up against the chair."

"Surely he didn't use that?" said Agnes.

"But what on earth was it *doing* there is what I want to know?" Ginger demanded.

"Maybe Bill's taken up boating," Guy offered but then coughed lightly to show the lameness of it, ". . . never cared for it though in school as I remember. *Tennis,* that was Bill's game—damn good he was too; on the varsity his last two years."

"I simply *cannot* make you understand what an absolute madman he was," said Ginger Horton. "There was something else on the chair too—a pair of *ice tongs* it looked like."

"Clamp, I suppose," murmured Grand.

" '*Better safe than sorry, eh, Mrs. Norton?*' he said to me like a perfect maniac, and then he said, 'Now I *don't* want you to swallow this!' and he dropped a *raw egg* into my mouth, grabbed up a lot of those weird instruments and rushed around the room, waving them over his head, and then out the door, *yelling at the top of his lungs!*"

"May have been called out on an emergency, you see," said Guy, "happens all too often in that business from what I've seen of it."

138

"What *was* he saying when he left, Ginger?" Agnes asked.

"*Saying?* He wasn't *saying* anything. He was simply yelling. '*Yaahh! Yaahh! Yaahh!*' it sounded like."

"How extraordinary," said Agnes.

"*What* was he saying?" Esther asked of Agnes.

" 'Yaahh, Yaahh,' " said Agnes quietly.

"Not like Bill," said Guy, shaking his head. "Must have been called out on emergency, only thing I can make of it."

"But surely the receptionist could have explained it all, my dear," said Agnes.

"There *was* no receptionist, I tell you!" said Ginger Horton irately. "There was no one but him—and a lot of fantastic instruments. And the chair was odd too! I'm lucky to have gotten out of there alive!"

"Did she swallow the egg?" asked Esther.

"Esther, for Heaven's sake!"

"What was that?" asked Grand, who seemed not to have heard.

"Esther wanted to know if Ginger had *swallowed* the egg," Agnes said.

"Certainly not!" said Ginger. "I spit it right out. Not at first, of course; I was in a state of complete shock. 'I *don't* want you to swallow this!' he said when he dropped it in, the maniac, so I just sat there in a state of pure shock while he raced around and around the room, screaming like a perfect madman!"

"Maybe it wasn't an egg," suggested Esther.

"What on earth do you mean?" demanded Ginger, quite beside herself. "It certainly *was* an egg—a raw egg! I *tasted* it and *saw* it, and some of the yellow got on my frock!"

"And then you filed a complaint with the authorities?" asked Agnes.

"Good Heavens, Agnes, I went straight to the police. Well, he could not be found! Disappeared without trace. Raving mad!"

"Bill Thorndike's no fool," said Grand loyally, "I'd stake my word on that."

"But *why* did he disappear like that, Guy?" asked Agnes.

"May have moved his offices to another part of the city, you see," Guy explained, "or out of the city altogether. I know Bill was awfully keen for the West Coast, as a matter of fact; couldn't get enough of California! Went out there every chance he could."

"*No*, he is not *anywhere* in this country," said Ginger Horton with considerable authority. "There is absolutely no *trace* of him."

"Don't tell me Bill's chucked the whole thing," said Grand reflectively, "given it all up and gone off to Bermuda or somewhere." He gave a soft tolerant chuckle. "Wouldn't surprise me too much though at that. I know Bill was awfully fond of *fishing* too, come to think of it. Yes, fishing and tennis—that was Bill Thorndike all right."

XVII

"But you just *cannot* go off like that, Guy," said Agnes, truly impatient with the boy now when he rose to leave. "Surely you shan't!"

"*Can* and *must*, my dears," Guy explained, kissing them both. "Flux, motion, growth, change—those are your great life principles. Best keep pace while we can."

He bent forward and took fat Ginger's hand in his own. "Yes, I'll be moving on, Ginger," he said with a warm smile for her, expansive now, perhaps in anticipation, "pushing down to Canaveral and out Los Alamos way!"

"Good Heavens," said Agnes, "in this dreadful heat? How silly!"

"Always on the go," purred Esther.

"It's wise to keep abreast," said Guy seriously. "I'll just nip down to Canaveral and see what's shaking on the space-scene, so to speak."

"Same old six-and-seven, Guy?" teased big Ginger, flashing up at him.

"Well, who can say?" admitted Guy frankly. "These are odd times—are, if I may say, times that try men's souls. Yet each of us does his *best*—who can say more?"

"Guy," said Ginger, squeezing his hand and sparkling up again on one monstrous surge of personality, "it *has* been fun!" Good-byes were her forte.

Guy gave a courtly nod, before turning to go, in deference, it seemed, to her beauty.

"My dear," he whispered, with a huskiness that made all the ladies tingle, "it has been . . . *inspiring*."

*

The S.S. *Magic Christian* was Grand's last major project—at least it was the last to be brought into open account. After that he began to taper off. However, he did like "keeping in touch," as he expressed it, and, for one thing, he bought himself a grocery store in New York City. Quite small, it was more or less indistinguishable from the several others in the neighborhood, and Grand put up a little sign in the window.

New Owner—New Policy
Big Get-Acquainted Sale

Grand was behind the counter himself, wearing a sort of white smock—not too unlike his big Vanity lab smock—when the store opened that evening.

His first customer was a man who lived next door to the store. He bought a carton of Grape-Ade.

"That will be three cents," said Grand.

"*How much?*" asked the man, with a frown.

"Three cents."

"Three *cents?* For six Grape-Ade? Are you kidding?"

"It's our two-for-one Get-Acquainted on Grape-Ade," said Grand. "It's new policy."

"Boy, *I'll* say it's new," said the man. "And how! Three *cents?* Okay by me, brother!" He slapped three cents on the counter. "There it is!" he said and still seemed amazed when Grand pushed the carton towards him.

"Call again," said Grand.

"That's some policy all right," said the man, looking back over his shoulder as he started for the door. At the door, however, he paused.

"Listen," he said, "do you sell it . . . uh, you know, by the *case?*"

"Well, yes," said Grand, "you would get some further reduction if you bought it by the case—not too much, of course; we're working on a fairly small profit-margin during the sale, you see and—"

"Oh, I'll pay the two-for-one all right. Christ! I just wanted to know if I could *get* a case at that price."

"Certainly, would you like a case?"

"Well, as a matter of fact, I could *use* more than one case . . ."

"How many cases could you use?"

"Well, uh . . . how many . . . how many have you *got?*"

"Could you use a thousand?"

"A *thousand?!?* A thousand cases of Grape-Ade?"

"Yes, I could give you . . . say, ten percent off on a thousand . . . and at twenty-four bottles to the case, twelve cents a case . . . would be one hundred and twenty dollars, minus ten percent, would be one hundred and eight . . . call it one-naught-five, shall we?"

"*No, no.* I couldn't use a thousand cases. Jesus! I meant, say, *ten* cases."

"That would be a dollar twenty."

"Right!" said the man. He slapped down a dollar twenty on the counter. "Boy, that's some policy you've got there!" he said.

"It's our Get-Acquainted policy," said Grand.

"It's some policy all right," said the man. "Have you got any other . . . *specials* on? You know, 'two-for-one,' that sort of thing?"

"Well, most of our items have been reduced for the Get-Acquainted."

The man hadn't noticed it before, but price tags were in evidence, and all prices had been sharply cut: milk, two cents a quart—butter, ten cents a pound—eggs, eleven cents a dozen—and so on.

The man looked wildly about him.

"How about cigarettes?"

"No, we decided we wouldn't carry cigarettes; since they've been linked, rather authoritatively, to cancer of the lung, we thought it wouldn't be exactly in the best of taste to sell them—being a *neighborhood* grocery, I mean to say."

"Uh-huh, well—listen, I'm just going home for a minute now to get a sack, or a . . . trunk, or maybe a truck . . . I'll be right back . . ."

Somehow the word spread through the neighborhood and in two hours the store was clean as a whistle.

The next day, a sign was on the empty store:

MOVED TO NEW LOCATION

And that evening, in another part of town, the same thing occurred—followed again by a quick change of location. The people who had experienced the phenomenon began to spend a good deal of their time each evening looking for the new location. And occasionally now, two such people meet—one who was at the big Get-Acquainted on West 4th Street, for example, and the other at the one on 139th—and so, presumably, they surmise not only that it wasn't a dream, but that it's still going on.

And some say it does, in fact, still go on—they say it accounts for the strange searching haste which can be seen in the faces, and especially the eyes, of people in the cities, every evening, just about the time now it starts really getting dark.

ABOUT THE AUTHOR

TERRY SOUTHERN was born in Alvarado, Texas. His first short stories were published in Paris in 1949 by *New-Story* and in 1953 by the *Paris Review*. A novel, *Flash and Filigree,* appeared in England in 1958 and was acclaimed by the *Observer* as one of the "twenty-one outstanding novels of the year."

Mr. Southern's short stories have recently been anthologized by David Burnett, editor of the *Best American Short Stories*. A portion of *The Magic Christian* received the Vanderbilt Prize for Humorous Fiction given in 1959 by the *Paris Review*.

Mr. Southern is married and lives in Connecticut.